TANGLED
IN
DECEIT

N. Viktoria

N. Viktoria/Alphazuriel Publishing
United States

Publisher's Note: This is a work of fiction. Names, characters, places, and incidents are a product of the author's imagination. Locales and public names are sometimes used for atmospheric purposes. Any resemblance to actual people, living or dead, or to businesses, companies, events, institutions, or locales is entirely coincidental.

Cover © 2023 Anchorage

Tangled in Deceit/ N.Viktoria -- 1st ed.
ISBN 9798396430259
-

CONTENTS

CHAPTER ONE

With a thoughtful air, Aaron gingerly nibbled at his lower lip. His back resting against the cushioned headboard, he found himself perched on the edge of his plush bed, lost in a mental tug-of-war. The question wasn't profound or life-altering, it was a simple one: to work or not to work?

He toyed with the idea of calling in and rescheduling his appointments, but that would only mean shifting his already hectic schedule to another time. As he gazed out of his bedroom window, the darkness of the early morning was slowly giving way to a faint glimmer of sunlight peeking through the clouds. It was as if the day itself was wrestling with the night, undecided on whether to fully embrace the dawn.

Sighing, Aaron sank back onto his bed, his features etched with resignation. He despised this predicament. He should have been up and preparing for work by now, but the thought of stepping out of his room filled him with apprehension. He knew all too well that his mother was an early riser, and he could hear her bustling about in the living room, occupied with tasks he hadn't assigned her. It was clear she was waiting for him to emerge from his sanctuary and continue the torment she had initiated the day before.

He let out a long breath, a shudder passing through his body as he recalled his mother's words. How could she have the audacity to play matchmaker and try to set him up with someone he didn't even know?

2

The mere thought made his lips curl with distaste. A junior Mrs. Montgomery? The idea seemed ludicrous to him. Mothers had an uncanny ability to frustrate their children in unimaginable ways.

"Aaron!" His name echoed through the house, jolting him out of his thoughts. He inwardly cursed himself for vocalizing his disdain. If he were in a war zone, he would have just revealed his position to the enemy. He chuckled at his own melodramatic musings.

"War front, huh?" he mused, shaking his head with a wry smile. He had to admit, he was engaged in a battle of sorts – a battle against his mother's relentless schemes and the invasion of his privacy.

"Aaron!" she called once more, her voice growing impatient. "Get yourself out here. I know you're awake."

He hesitated, considering his options. Going out there meant subjecting himself to her meddling and the inevitable arguments that would follow. Yet, staying hidden in his room would only prolong the conflict. With a resigned sigh, he pushed himself off the bed, mustering the courage to face whatever awaited him beyond that bedroom door.

Mustering the most cheerful voice he could at this ungodly hour, he called out, "Good morning, Mom."

A chuckle echoed back to him, laced with a certain satisfaction that Aaron knew all too well. "Morning to you, son."

He found himself chuckling along, despite the intricate dance of annoyance and amusement playing in his heart. His mother was nothing if not persistent, he'd give her that. Even with her incessant scheming and matchmaking, she somehow always found a way to alleviate his exasperation, even if just slightly.

But no amount of persuasion or sweet talk could make him budge. The very thought of a blind date set up by her was enough to make his stomach turn. A forced smile, awkward silence, and polite niceties - it wasn't him, and he was sure any woman could see right through it.

"You heading off to work, aren't you?" His mother's voice sliced through his thoughts, bringing him back to reality.

"Yes, Mom," Aaron confirmed. Honestly, the prospect of a long day at work seemed more appealing than sitting at home, enduring another session of her praising how exquisite, elegant, and perfect her friend's daughter was.

"Well then, spruce up quick, I'm making breakfast already." Her voice was soft, almost innocent. But he knew better.

The mere thought of breakfast made his mouth water. He missed the intoxicating aromas of her cooking that used to fill the house every morning, the savory and sweet flavors of home that he had long forgotten amidst hurried mornings and rushed breakfasts.

His morning routine was swift and by six, he was all set to face the day. As he moved towards the living room, he began strategizing the morning's showdown. He'd keep his breakfast brief, barely ten minutes. He'd eat just enough to keep him from having to talk too much and maybe even pretend not to hear her if she tried to push the conversation in that direction.

At precisely ten past six, he'd be out the door. By the time he returned from work, hopefully late, she'd be sound asleep. With luck, she'd tire herself out eventually, accept his reluctance, and head back home.

The plan seemed foolproof. After all, she wouldn't dare to invite this 'perfect' daughter-in-law-to-be without discussing it with him first, right?

His train of thought screeched to a halt as he stepped out of his bedroom. His eyes widened in surprise as they fell upon the dining table, meticulously laid as if for a grand feast.

"What?" he croaked, confusion and disbelief gnawing at him. "Are we having a party, Mom?" A sickening realization dawned on him. Had his mom disregarded his feelings and invited her chosen daughter-in-law overnight without his knowledge? His heart pounded in his chest as he braced for her answer.

Her laughter filled the room, a warm, lilting sound that banished his worries momentarily. "Don't be absurd, son," she dismissed him with a wave of her hand.

"Why all this food, Mom?" Aaron asked, concern tinging his voice. If she kept up with this rate of extravagant meals, he'd be heading for bankruptcy sooner than he thought.

"I couldn't figure out what you'd like for breakfast, given that you decided to lock yourself away. So, I thought I'd prepare a variety," she shrugged nonchalantly. "You can always take the leftovers as lunch for work."

He closed his eyes briefly, a sigh escaping his lips. "Mom, if this continues, I'll have to go grocery shopping every other day. I simply don't have the time." Surely, she could've just asked him what he wanted, instead of practically cooking through his entire pantry?

His gaze narrowed suspiciously at her. Was this her way of getting back at him for refusing the date with... what was her name again? He was certain his mother had mentioned it, but ever since she dropped the matchmaking bomb, his mind had been in a perpetual state of chaos.

9

She wore a content smile as if privy to his inner turmoil. "That's good. But ensure you do your shopping when Samantha is around. It would provide an excellent opportunity for you two to bond."

Samantha. That was the name. But he couldn't care less.

His frown deepened at her suggestion. "I've already told you, Mom, I have a girlfriend."

"Until I meet this mysterious girlfriend of yours, my dear son, I will continue with my matchmaking schemes." Her voice held a hint of challenge.

With a resigned sigh, he pulled out a chair and slumped into it. So much for his strategic breakfast plan. His mother, once again, had outmaneuvered him.

The hands of the clock had already swept past the fifteen-minute mark, his dream of a ten-minute breakfast shattered. As he stared at the veritable feast before him, he realized he'd have to eat heartily now; he certainly had no intention of carrying a lunch box to work like a schoolboy.

He couldn't help but snort at the thought. Here he was, a man of thirty-two, still being treated like a child by his mother, who didn't hesitate to remind him of his age while forcing him to live like a teenager.

But as he dug into the meal, his thoughts strayed to a more pressing concern. He still had to convince Elena to pose as his girlfriend, and the clock was ticking ruthlessly. The thought of the impending challenge made his breakfast taste a little less delicious.

***

Elena took a deep breath, trying to steady her emotions as she stood in front of her full-length mirror. Her hands unconsciously smoothed out invisible creases on her dress, a futile attempt to calm her inner turmoil. The events of the previous day, the embarrassment she had endured because of Aaron, lingered in her mind, leaving her feeling helpless and vulnerable.

If it were up to her, she wouldn't go to work today. The thought of facing her colleagues after the ordeal Aaron had put her through made her cringe. But she had no alternative at the moment, so she sighed resignedly and reminded herself to muster whatever confidence she could. With a heavy heart, she left her apartment and headed to the office.

As she walked into the company, Elena avoided making eye contact with her colleagues. She kept her head down, deliberately trying to shield herself from their judgmental gazes. She knew exactly what they were thinking, and she wanted to spare herself the pity, curiosity, and possible mockery that would be directed her way.

"Elena," Allyssa called out to her, but Elena quickened her pace, pretending not to have heard. She didn't stop until she reached her office, finally finding a moment of respite as she sank into her chair. She let out a relieved sigh, momentarily free from the scrutiny of others.

Picking up the calendar, she prepared to go through Aaron's appointments for the day when her phone rang. Seeing Sabrina's name on the caller ID brought a faint smile to her face. Perhaps a good conversation with Sabrina would help lift her spirits and distract her from the sour mood that had enveloped her.

"Hey, girl," Elena greeted, though the usual enthusiasm in her voice was noticeably absent. The reminder of being in the office dampened her excitement, as she knew that any conversation could be short-lived. She was all too aware that any employee, especially those who enjoyed spreading rumors, could walk in under the pretense of checking on her and linger around just to gather information to share with the eager ears waiting to know her every move.

Even though she hadn't seen Aaron yet, she knew he was in the office, and the thought of him calling her at any moment sent a strange mix of anticipation and fear coursing through her veins. She silently hoped that Sabrina had some good news to share, something she could hold onto throughout the day.

As Elena heard the door from one of the neighboring offices close, she jumped, instinctively holding her breath. Moments later, she scolded herself for getting so worked up. She couldn't let every noise send her into a panic.

"Are you happy, girl?" Sabrina's voice sounded subdued, lacking its usual energy. Elena furrowed her brow, her mind racing with assumptions as she wondered why Sabrina wasn't her usual self. She hoped this call wouldn't bring more bad news about Cole.

She scoffed at her own conspiracy theories, reminding herself that she had been the one to make a fuss about her own life. It was only natural for Sabrina to sound concerned and subdued.

"I'm fine," Elena replied, injecting some forced enthusiasm into her voice for Sabrina's sake. "Did you call just to check up on me? That's sweet of you, Sabrina."

There was a hesitation on the other end of the line, causing Elena's guard to go up. She bit her lip, nervously fumbling with her fingers as she waited for Sabrina to speak. Deep down, she knew there was more to this call than just a friendly check-in. Sabrina wouldn't have hesitated if there wasn't something else on her mind.

"Sabrina," Elena finally said, breaking the silence that had grown too uncomfortable. She needed to end the call before Aaron chose to summon her. She stole a glance at his office door, a silent reminder of his surprising absence so far. Aaron surely knew she was in the building by now.

She sighed, running her hand through her hair, only to remember she had arranged her long thick waves into a tight bun. The day was unfolding in an extraordinarily peculiar way. Sabrina's missing pep and Aaron's unusual silence were abnormal, adding to her feeling of unease.

"I think I'll call you back...or maybe just text you," Sabrina said at last, her voice shaky.

A text? Elena couldn't help but let out a derisive snort loud enough for Sabrina to hear. Text messages were an easy way out, a method for delivering uncomfortable news without having to face immediate reactions. She had a feeling Sabrina had more to say and Elena steeled herself for whatever was coming her way.

Elena regarded Sabrina as courageous, so her hesitance now was perplexing. "Go ahead and spill it, Sabrina," she urged, curious and somewhat apprehensive. Sabrina, who often came across as stoic, had a soft spot for delivering unpleasant news, and her discomfort now was an ominous sign.

Sabrina sighed, and Elena could almost visualize her nervously biting her nails on the other end. "Your stepfather took out a loan," Sabrina finally managed to say.

Elena was on the verge of laughing. This was what had Sabrina worried? She questioned why this matter was of any relevance to her, let alone why Sabrina deemed it significant enough to share. Elena had never had a soft spot for Thomas, her mother's second husband, who came into their lives following her father's death. To her, Thomas was a slick, sly old man whose true character seemed apparent to everyone but her late mother.

His smug demeanor and overconfident air had always irked Elena. The thought of such an attitude instantly brought to mind another person she knew too well. She gave a derisive snort, musing over the irony.

Her lack of concern must have been evident because Sabrina cleared her throat, adding, "Thomas listed you as a guarantor for the loan before he vanished. Now the loan sharks are after you."

The revelation felt like a bucket of cold water over Elena's head. She sat rigid in her chair, phone gripped in her hand, as the words echoed in her mind. Her personal estrangement from Thomas would mean nothing to the loan sharks. The fact that they hadn't exchanged words in years would be a mere footnote in the unfolding drama.

She let out a soft curse under her breath. As if her life wasn't already spiraling, this added development felt like a knockout punch. Just when she thought things couldn't possibly get any worse, they had. Now, she wasn't just dealing with office gossip and Aaron's peculiar behavior; she was potentially on the radar of loan sharks, all thanks to a stepfather she barely tolerated. How much more could she possibly endure?

CHAPTER TWO

She swiped at her face, brushing away the threatening tear that lingered on the edge of her eyelid. All she yearned for in that moment was the comfort of her own home. She could lock herself away, surrounded by a fortress of tissue boxes, and determine just how many she could fill with her tears. Perhaps she would even break a Guinness World Record for the sheer quantity of tissues used by a single person. Such thoughts provided a temporary distraction from the mounting frustrations in her life, especially the audacity of Thomas to borrow money from loan sharks and then vanish into thin air.

Knowing Thomas as she did, she had no doubt that he had gambled away the borrowed money. The loan sharks he had dealt with must have been ruthless if he had resorted to fleeing after losing their funds. And now, those same loan sharks were hot on her trail.

"Ah!" she groaned, clenching her fists in frustration. If only she had taken up martial arts when she had the chance, and if only she had enough money to escape this predicament. She yearned to search for Thomas and unleash her fury upon him, to make him pay for the chaos he had brought into her life.

But instead, she had to endure the drudgery of the office. Suppressing her emotions, she reminded herself that her detestable boss sat mere meters away. As if conjured by her thoughts, the connecting door between their offices swung open, and he stepped into her space.

24

She pressed her lips together, assuming a blank expression to mask any trace of her inner turmoil. All she desired was to get through the day and return to the solace of her own sanctuary.

"Good morning, sir," she greeted him as politely as she could muster, pretending to have forgotten the embarrassing incident they had shared during their last encounter.

"Good morning, Elena," he replied, his tone unexpectedly warm and different.

Her head snapped up at the sound of his voice, her eyes widening with a mixture of surprise and dread as she noticed the unfamiliar smile adorning his face. Instantly, her guard went up, her narrowed eyes scrutinizing him. It was clear to her that Aaron had some ulterior motive.

Perhaps he had schemed another prank, but this time, she vowed to be prepared.

Already burdened by stress, she refused to allow another prank to break her down. She would be strong. No tears would be shed, unlike the vulnerable display she had exhibited recently. Aaron wouldn't gain the satisfaction of witnessing her distress.

"I was just about to bring in your schedule and the files requiring your signature, sir," she stated, rifling through the papers scattered across her desk and searching through the drawers. She groaned inwardly as she realized she had inadvertently set herself up for another reprimand. However, she couldn't entirely fault herself; it was Aaron's fault for his thoughtless actions that had driven her to flee the office in embarrassment without tidying up.

He approached her desk, tapping lightly until he had captured her attention. "I'm not here for that, Elena."

She halted, her eyes widening as she arched her eyebrows at him. A boulder settled in her heart, leaving her with a sense of foreboding. She took a slow, deliberate breath, hating how her anxiety threatened to constrict her breathing.

"I'm sorry, Elena," he blurted out, his face turning beet red as the words tumbled out.

"What?" she squeaked, caught off guard by his unexpected apology. Her eyebrows shot up, revealing her surprise.

"I said I was sorry," he repeated, his voice tinged with sincerity.

She shook her head, trying to process the situation. "Of course, I heard you the first time. I was just... shocked."

He chuckled; the sound laced with a hint of self-awareness. "Surprised that I could be sorry? Let's just say I've grown up."

She snorted, unable to contain her skepticism. Overnight transformation? That seemed like quite the miraculous change to accept without question. She doubted his sincerity, despite the appearance of remorse. "What do you want?"

He stared at her, a look of surprise crossing his face, although he knew he shouldn't be taken aback by her response. A smile crept onto his lips, pulling at the corners.

He realized he had made the right choice by approaching Elena. She saw through him, understood him on a deeper level. His mother was perceptive, and he couldn't bring just any girl into their lives. She would undoubtedly see through his charade in an instant, banishing both of them from the house and ushering in Samantha before he could say Jack.

If he didn't want to jeopardize his chance of convincing his mother that he truly had a girlfriend, he might as well invest in a new suit for an eventual wedding with Samantha. But now, he had found his pretend girlfriend, and he had to persuade Elena to play the part. Yet, as he stared at her, a nervous exhale escaping his lips, he couldn't believe how on edge he felt around her. He hadn't experienced such nerves when they first met or even when he asked her out in college.

He had found his solution, but now he needed to convince her to become his girlfriend. It wouldn't be an easy task, he knew, especially judging by the way she glared at him, her eyes shooting daggers in his direction.

"What do you want, Aaron?" she asked, her impatience seeping into her voice.

He swallowed hard, feeling his tongue tie itself into knots under her penetrating gaze. Talking to Elena suddenly seemed more daunting than he had anticipated. He gathered his thoughts, trying to find the right words.

"Be my girlfriend," he blurted out, immediately wincing at the realization of what he had said.

His discomfort grew as he cleared his throat, shifting his feet uneasily on the tiled office floor. Her incredulous stare made him feel as though he had sprouted horns, leaving him questioning his own audacity.

She blinked at him, momentarily taken aback. "What?" she snorted, her choice of words tinged with disbelief.

He cleared his throat again, attempting to regain his composure. "I'm not saying I'm in love with you or asking you to be my official girlfriend..."

"Of course, you aren't," she sneered, interrupting him with a touch of sarcasm.

He ignored her skepticism and continued, his words filled with urgency. "All I need is a pretend girlfriend, Elena. Someone to ward off my mom's attempts to arrange a marriage I don't want. And I can't think of anyone else but you, considering our history. You would be able to convince my mom."

She shrugged dismissively, a hint of indifference in her voice. "And you think I care about convincing your mom? Why should I bother if you end up in an arranged marriage? It's none of my concern, Aaron."

"Elena, please," he pleaded, his desperation palpable. "I need you."

Of all the scenarios she had imagined, him apologizing and begging her to save him from an unwanted relationship wasn't one of them. Unconsciously, she burst into laughter, her body shaking with the force of it, her throat echoing with the sound.

She continued to laugh, feeling the weight of stress and anxiety wash away with each burst of laughter. It was liberating, a much-needed release. Aaron, she thought, should consider a career in comedy rather than being a business executive. He might have a knack for it, she sneered mockingly.

He stood there, his face flushed with embarrassment. With a frustrated grunt, he turned and walked back to his office, unable to bear her laughter any longer.

He deserved that, he thought as she slowly composed herself, the laughter subsiding.

Taking a deep breath, Aaron contemplated his next move. Aaron needed to secure her participation before the end of the workday so that he could confidently inform his mother about his girlfriend's availability.

He couldn't keep bluffing or he would dig himself into a deeper hole of lies.

As he settled back into his chair, contemplating how best to convince her, his phone rang, startling him out of his thoughts. He stared at the caller ID in disbelief.

Max? His carefree cousin rarely called unless there was a reason. Aaron was skeptical, wondering what had prompted the call. The last time Max had reached out, he had gotten himself into trouble and needed Aaron's help to bail him out.

Rolling his eyes, Aaron hoped this call wasn't going to be another request for rescue. He was hardly in the mood and had no desire to play the role of a savior.

"I'm not sure this call is for me," Aaron teased.

"Ouch, cousin, you hurt me," Max chuckled. "Can't I call just because I miss you?"

Aaron laughed, feeling a sense of relief as the embarrassment from earlier began to fade away. "I highly doubt that. You don't just call for no reason unless there are boobs involved."

"Fuck off, dude," Max laughed. He cleared his throat. "You should have warned me that you were about to leave me in the bachelor zone."

Aaron's heart skipped a beat. He couldn't believe his mother was already spreading the news about Samantha, a woman he hadn't even agreed to marry.

He coughed lightly, pretending to be oblivious. "I'm not sure I understand what you mean."

Max snorted. "I called your mom to say hello this morning, and she informed me that you have a girlfriend. You didn't tell me, dude. I thought I was your best friend."

Max's hurt was evident in his voice, but Aaron knew that his cousin didn't mean any harm. He let out a heavy sigh, trying to find the right words to explain the complicated situation.

"It's... it's complicated, dude," Aaron finally replied, his voice filled with frustration and resignation.

Max's tone softened, his concern evident. "I understand, Aaron. Just remember that I'm here for you. And hey, when you bring her over, I'd love to meet her. Let me know when that happens."

Aaron's heart sank. His mother was already spreading the news, creating expectations and inviting a crowd to meet a girl he didn't even have yet. "Thanks, Max. I'll talk to you later, man," he said, quickly ending the call.

He felt a sense of urgency coursing through him. Time was slipping away, and he needed to return to Elena's office to convince her to play the role of his girlfriend, even if it meant spending the entire day trying to persuade her.

Jumping to his feet, Aaron briskly made his way back to Elena's office, his mind racing with thoughts of how he could win her over and ensure that his elaborate charade would succeed.

CHAPTER THREE

Elena gently dabbed at her face, her hand moving with care to wipe away the streaks of tears. She couldn't believe how unexpectedly funny Aaron had turned out to be. It was clear that she didn't know him as well as he had thought.

"Pretend girlfriend?" she mused, releasing another amused snort that threatened to escalate into laughter. Shaking her head, she sighed, attempting to regain control over her amusement. Thankfully, she hadn't applied any makeup before coming to work. The tears from her laughing session would have undoubtedly smeared her foundation, washed off her mascara, and left her face in disarray.

The thought of presenting a disheveled appearance to Aaron, in a desperate attempt to dissuade him from asking her to be his girlfriend, seemed like an arduous undertaking she was not willing to endure. Going around with a stained dress and a smeared face just to chase off a man was simply too much trouble.

Yes, she was grateful she hadn't bothered with makeup that morning.

Deciding to occupy her mind with any immediate task at hand, Elena sought something to keep herself busy. If she had work to focus on, she could easily redirect her thoughts away from what had made her laugh in the first place. Grabbing a pen and a blank sheet of paper, she began to scribble her thoughts away. Since she had no new assignments for the day, she engaged in this impromptu activity.

Her boss who was supposed to assign her tasks seemed to have gone rogue, leaving Elena uncertain about approaching his office while she was still trying to regain control over her laughter. Bursting out laughing in his presence would surely result in her swift dismissal despite their past romance.

Although Aaron might have requested her assistance as a pretend girlfriend to extricate himself from a ridiculous situation, choosing to ignore her initial fits of laughter due to the mutual shock they had experienced, she doubted he would tolerate a repeat performance in his office. The Aaron she currently knew would not be able to withstand a fresh dose of embarrassment, regardless of how much he needed her help.

With determination, Elena continued to write, aiming to divert her attention away from Aaron's proposition. As she blew out a breath, she gradually regained her composure and sank into her chair, allowing the pen to slip from her grasp as she stared into the empty space before her.

Reflecting on the unexpected troubles that each person carried, Elena realized that she shouldn't have laughed at Aaron. After all, she, too, had her own problems that she hadn't asked for. She felt a pang of guilt for finding amusement in his predicament. Everyone had their own share of unexpected burdens to bear.

Elena sighed in despair, her hands pressed against her temples as she pondered the state of her life. She quickly corrected herself, realizing that she knew what she wanted to do with her life. The real question was how to fix the mess she found herself in.

The office door swung open once again, and her gaze lifted to see Aaron entering. She pursed her lips, grateful that she had already regained control over her laughter. "What do you want now?" she sighed, her gaze flickering toward the intercom on her desk. "There's the intercom, Aaron."

He pulled out the chair across from her, settling into it, his hands resting on the desk as he leaned forward to meet her gaze. "You already know why I'm here, Elena."

She snorted, not falling for his soft tone. Searching his eyes, she saw the pleading look in them. His big blue eyes held an adorability that threatened to break through her defenses, reminding her of how captivating they could be.

43

A memory flashed through her mind, a recollection of the last time his eyes had softened and sparkled at her. She almost let out a moan, feeling a flush of embarrassment as she realized where her thoughts were heading. Rubbing her legs together discreetly under the desk, she was grateful that he couldn't see her body's reaction.

The memory felt vivid and tangible, eliciting a physical response that surprised her. Just sitting in front of him, having him gaze at her, aroused sensations and desires from their past intimate encounters. It was yet another reason to dismiss his ridiculous idea from her mind.

If she could become aroused simply from a memory of their past relationship, what would happen if she had to be physically close to him and pretend to be his

44

girlfriend? It would ignite sparks and inevitably lead to trouble. No, it was better to avoid such complications than to pray for deliverance from a situation she willingly walked into.

"No, Aaron," she asserted firmly. "It's not going to work."

"Elena," he pleaded, his pained groan tugging at her heart.

Come on, Elena. Since when did you become so weak? She scolded herself for succumbing to weak knees just because he looked adorable. She mentally smacked herself, refusing to let her thoughts drift to a place where she had been vulnerable before. The physical sensations were overwhelming, and she knew she couldn't afford to lose control in his presence.

She resolved to remain seated until he left her office, avoiding any further temptation. Ah, if only she had resigned from her job when she had the chance. From the very beginning, she had been fighting against the rekindling of her attraction to him, and this recent revelation, even though he didn't mean it sincerely, only intensified the struggle.

And that was the cruelest part of it all. She knew he didn't mean it. As she stared at him, she became more convinced that this was just business as usual for him, devoid of genuine emotions.

Her brain acknowledged that Aaron's intention was merely to avoid an unwanted relationship, but her body seemed to have a mind of its own. It had already melted into a puddle at the mere look he had given her.

Attempting to regain control, she reminded herself of his recent unpleasant behavior towards her and the emotional ache she had experienced when she returned home. She sighed with relief as the sensations subsided, her body no longer squirming beneath her legs, memories of the physical connection with Aaron still fresh in her mind.

Clearing her throat, she spoke with a clearer and firmer voice. "No, Aaron. I don't want to be your girlfriend, whether it's fake or real. I've moved on from the past. I'm not certain I would be suitable for the role you're proposing," she carefully explained, ensuring he grasped every word.

She chuckled inwardly at her choice of words. Had she truly moved on from the past? Well, she could certainly tell that to her wet panties. She knew she had lied

47

about leaving the past behind, but he didn't need to know that.

"I'll double your salary," he offered, attempting to entice her.

She snorted, realizing the futility of a higher salary when she planned to leave the job soon. "Not interested," she replied firmly.

"I'll give you anything you want, Elena. Just name it," he persisted.

Your heart? The thought flickered through her mind, prompting an eye roll at the idea of his heart being part of the bargain.

"Name your price, girl," he urged.

She snorted, fully aware that his heart wouldn't be part of any deal. The words "name your price" echoed in her head, and suddenly she saw an opportunity. She could ask for what she truly needed. A blank check had been handed to her, and it would be foolish not to take advantage of it.

"Do you mean that?" she asked, her eyes gleaming with excitement.

"Yes," he replied, relieved that she was considering his offer.

"Well," she began, her voice tinged with a newfound confidence, "I'm sure you know a lot of people in law enforcement in this area."

"Yes," he nodded, his eyes narrowing with suspicion. "Why? Are you in trouble?"

She sighed, hesitant to reveal the whole truth. "Maybe. Maybe not. I need protection from a group of individuals. I want you to promise me that you'll be there for me when I need you."

She skirted around the details, feeling a sense of embarrassment about divulging that she had dated someone who turned out to be dangerous and was now relentlessly pursuing her. She also didn't know the loan sharks' identities, but she had heard that they were searching for her, holding her accountable for Thomas's disappearance.

Curiosity piqued, Aaron inquired, "Who are they?"

With a resigned sigh, she realized he wouldn't relent. "Loan sharks. Thomas used me to borrow money and then disappeared. I don't know who they are, but I've heard that they are looking for me and will hold me responsible if they can't find Thomas."

"Thomas has always been trouble," Aaron groaned, a hint of frustration in his voice.

Elena nodded, acknowledging the shared sentiment. "It's unfortunate that he hasn't changed."

"Remember that night when he got drunk and called you while we were together, insulting you?" Aaron recalled, a hint of amusement in his tone.

She chuckled, unable to forget that memorable evening. "I can't erase that from my memory." And what we had been up to that night before his untimely call, she thought, her cheeks flushing with a hint of embarrassment.

As their eyes locked, an unspoken agreement passed between them to leave those memories unspoken. They both knew what had transpired, the intensity of their connection on that night lingering in their minds.

Elena swallowed hard, her gaze fixed on Aaron, aware that he, too, was thinking about the passionate encounter they had shared. This was a complicated situation. She doubted that becoming his girlfriend, even if it was fake, would be a wise decision. However, she couldn't ignore the opportunity presented by the blank check he had figuratively thrown her way.

She needed his protection, and beyond that, she needed financial security. She could ask for a substantial amount of money, enough to support herself and save for the future when she eventually resigned and sought new job opportunities.

Breaking the spell between them, Aaron blinked, licked his lips, and cleared his throat. "Is that all?"

"Of course not," Elena replied, a mischievous grin spreading across her face. "For each date I go on with you to convince your mom, you will pay me the equivalent of my monthly salary."

He stared at her in surprise, impressed by her negotiation skills. "So, you want a month's salary for each day you pretend to be my girlfriend?"

"Yes. Any problem with that?" she challenged.

He chuckled, realizing why she had rejected his initial offer to double her salary. If he agreed to her plan, he would be paying her significantly more than he had initially proposed. Her determination caught him off guard, but he couldn't deny the fairness in her request, considering the situation.

She scowled at his hesitation. "You can forget about it if you can't agree to the deal," she bluffed, well aware that he wouldn't reject her offer. She could sense his desperation, and it was only fitting that she used it to her advantage, just as he had used his position against her.

Elena couldn't help but feel a surge of satisfaction as the tables turned in her favor.

"I'll take it," Aaron said with a smile, raising his hands in surrender.

He hoped his mother would be convinced sooner rather than later, sparing him from multiple instances of pretending to be in a relationship. While he was wealthy, he didn't want to bankrupt himself just to avoid an unwanted marriage.

"Deal," Elena affirmed, a genuine smile spreading across her face.

"Deal," he grunted, shaking his head in amusement. "Let me have your phone."

"Why?" Elena narrowed her gaze at Aaron, suspicion evident in her eyes. Was he trying to play yet another prank on her?

He snorted, amused by her reaction. "Don't you think it's strange for a boyfriend not to have his girlfriend's personal contact?"

"Oh!" Elena blushed, realizing the practicality of his request. She handed him her phone, unlocking it for him.

As Aaron inserted his number into her phone and dialed it to ensure it was saved, he furrowed his brow, noticing that she had started locking her phone. It made him question whether he truly knew her as well as he had thought.

Returning the phone to her, he said, "Here, you have your phone back. My personal contact is already saved." He quickly saved her contact on his phone as well.

Elena gasped when she saw what he had named himself on her phone. She raised her head to glare at him. "My love?"

He shrugged, a mischievous glint in his eyes. "That's what you used to save my contact as."

"That was then," she refuted, her tone slightly defensive. "When I was your girlfriend."

"But you're my girlfriend now," he chuckled, finding amusement in their banter.

She fell silent, blushing at his words, her lips caught between her teeth as she reluctantly admitted that he was right.

"Don't bite your lips, Elena," he groaned, a hint of desire in his voice. "You make me want to kiss you so badly."

Her eyes widened, her lip slipping out from between her teeth, her body reacting to his words.

Leaning forward, Aaron focused on her moistened lips, a mischievous glimmer in his eyes. "Should we kiss each other now? Just to see if we still have that chemistry between us," he suggested nonchalantly, though deep down, he longed to taste her again. The image of her walking into his office as his personal assistant had ignited a desire within him from day one.

She scoffed, determined to keep the situation under control. "You didn't pay for a kiss. You paid for a fake girlfriend," she retorted, emphasizing the word "fake."

Aaron chuckled, recognizing the need to redirect the conversation to safer territory. The tension in the air was becoming palpable, and he was feeling its effects more than he had anticipated.

A tiny groan escaped his lips as desire stirred within him, making his body respond. He shouldn't have mentioned kissing. Now, all he could think about was ravishing her mouth and unraveling the tight bun that adorned her head, tangling his fingers in her hair as they surrendered to their passion.

"What would you have saved my contact as? Boss?" Aaron asked, attempting to regain control of his thoughts before they manifested into actions he might regret.

She snickered. "Boss is a suitable term. I would have saved your contact with a far less endearing term."

He laughed. "I'm glad I saved my contact myself. Don't change it."

"Yes, boss," she teased, a mischievous glimmer in her eyes.

He scowled playfully. "Just make sure not to slip up and call me that when we're with my mom."

"Don't worry. You shouldn't treat me like trash at work anymore either," she replied, her tone laced with determination. "No matter how much you pay me, any more mistreatment from you and I'll leave you to find another girl."

"Noted," Aaron said, a smile tugging at his lips. "Make sure to answer my call tonight."

"Tonight?" Elena gasped, her heart skipping a beat at the sudden realization that their charade had already begun.

"Your work has begun, Miss Williams," he chuckled. "We need to go over our story

60

tonight because we're meeting my mom tomorrow." With that, he walked out of her office.

Elena blew out a breath as Aaron exited. Wow, that had been intense. Why did he have to bring up the possibility of kissing? She had almost given him permission to do that and more.

If she was going to navigate this fake relationship with Aaron without losing herself, she needed someone to keep her grounded, someone who knew about their past relationship, the reasons for their breakup, and her reluctance to get involved with him again.

Who better to call than Sabrina—the person who had witnessed their relationship firsthand and understood the complexities surrounding it?

With a deep breath, Elena picked up her phone and dialed Sabrina's number, ready to seek her friend's guidance and support as she embarked on this challenging journey with Aaron.

CHAPTER FOUR

Elena checked her reflection in the mirror for the thousandth time that night, realizing that she was nervous. She had chosen a stunning outfit that highlighted her curves while exuding elegance. She wore a knee-length, figure-hugging dress in a rich shade of royal blue. The dress had a modest V-neckline that accentuated her décolletage, and the sleeves gracefully covered her shoulders. The fabric had a subtle sheen, adding a touch of sophistication to her ensemble.

The dress featured a cinched waistline, emphasizing her hourglass figure, and gently flowed down, skimming over her curves. The tailored silhouette hugged her curves in all the right places, allowing her to radiate beauty from within.

To complete the look, Elena paired the dress with sleek black pumps, adding a touch of sophistication and elongating her legs. She opted for minimalistic gold accessories, including delicate hoop earrings and a dainty necklace that rested elegantly on her collarbone.

Elena styled her hair in loose, voluminous curls that cascaded down her shoulders, framing her face with an air of effortless glamour. She opted for a natural and radiant makeup look, enhancing her features with a touch of bronzer, a soft smoky eye, and a bold, deep red lip color that complemented her skin tone beautifully.

As Elena admired her reflection, she couldn't help but feel the familiar flutter of nervous anticipation. Aaron would be picking her up in the next ten minutes and she was as nervous as an innocent bride on her first night with her husband.

"Come on, Elena. It's just acting. It's a job," she encouraged herself. "You were as good as any professional back in high school."

The doorbell rang and she exhaled, picking her purse off the drawer. This was it, Elena. Let's go.

She stepped out and almost lost her footing at the sight of Aaron. He looked dashing in a tailored navy-blue suit, the fabric hugging his frame in all the right places. The jacket was expertly cut, accentuating his broad shoulders and slender waist. The fine details, such as the slim lapels and perfectly aligned buttons, showcased the garment's quality craftsmanship. A crisp white dress shirt adorned his torso, its collar peeking out from under the suit jacket with elegant precision.

Completing the ensemble was a deep burgundy tie, intricately woven with a subtle pattern that added a touch of intrigue to the overall look. The tie was expertly knotted, a testament to Aaron's attention to detail. A silver tie clip adorned with a tasteful design secured the tie in place, adding a sophisticated touch.

His trousers, matching the navy blue hue of the suit jacket, were impeccably tailored to his legs. The slim fit gave him a modern and polished appearance, while the pressed creases added a refined touch. A sleek black leather belt, fastened neatly around his waist, completed the ensemble.

But that wasn't the problem. It was the way he was looking at her.

He reached out to hold her steady and she felt warm all over where his hand had touched her skin. She scolded herself for not wearing a full sleeved dress.

"You look beautiful, Elena." His voice was alluring.

She swallowed and pulled herself away from his grasp. "Thanks." She said, turning to the door to lock it.

Her hands began to shake and she struggled with inserting the key into the door hole, fully aware that he was behind her and roving his eyes all over her body.

"Here, let me." He said, moving closer and took the key from her hand. "Seems like I make you nervous."

She snorted. "Don't feed your ego. I'm just nervous about meeting the mother of someone who is not actually my boyfriend."

He didn't respond to what she had said and handed her key back to her. "Shall we?"

She nodded and followed him to where his car was.

"We are going to your house, right?"

"Sadly, no." He sighed, his hands tightening on the wheels. "My mom went back home yesterday before I got back from work. She said she would like the other members of the family to meet you as well."

"What?" Elena gasped and started to hyperventilate. The air in the car wasn't enough and her head started to ache. She wished he would stop the car.

"I'm sorry, Elena." He apologized, placing a hand on her lap.

The touch sent a jolt through her body, and she felt a mixture of comfort and confusion. Her mind was a whirlwind of thoughts, but she tried to focus on his words.

"This is bad."

"I know."

She sighed. She would have to convince not just his mother that they were in love but a whole lot of others.

"You can still do it, right?" He asked.

She smiled, knowing that he was nervous as well about the outcome of the day. "I'm

69

sure we would survive the outcome of the day, baby."

His head snapped towards her, and she gasped as he suddenly pressed on the brake, right in the middle of the road.

"Aaron." She breathed. "Do you want to kill us?"

"Say it again." He smiled at her.

"What?" She frowned at him. "That we would survive the day?"

"No." He grinned, shaking his head. "Call me baby again."

She chuckled. "I will only be saying this, so you don't get a ticket as you are causing traffic."

He chuckled. "Just say it."

"Baby." She repeated.

He grinned and stepped on the gas. "I love the sound of that."

"Get used to it. I will be calling you that when we get to your mom's house. It wouldn't look nice if I call you baby and then you choke on your food. You will be giving us away with that."

He laughed. "I can always tell them that I am so in love with you that hearing you say that never ceases to stop my heart."

"Of course, you have a way with words." She said and turned towards the window.

He frowned, wondering what she meant by the words but didn't want to ask to avoid ruining the mood.

As they drove through the upscale neighborhood of Palm Beach, Elena couldn't help but admire the luxurious houses and well-manicured gardens they passed by. It was a stark contrast to her own humble neighborhood, but she reminded herself that this was all part of the act.

"Are you ready for this?" Aaron asked, his voice filled with a mix of excitement and nervousness.

Elena took a deep breath and nodded. "I'm ready. We've got this."

"We are here," Aaron announced, driving into a stunning building that filled Elena with a mixture of awe and nervousness. She reminded herself that she would be meeting Aaron's mom and possibly other family members.

As Aaron parked the car, he hissed at Elena to wait before getting out. She raised an eyebrow, curious about his sudden urgency.

"What's the matter?" she asked, turning to him.

"My cousin, Max, is on his way here. Stay in the car, and let me get the door for you," Aaron whispered in a low tone.

Elena winced inwardly. The show had started the moment they arrived, leaving them no time to catch their breath.

"Come on out, sweetheart," Aaron grinned as he opened the car door for her.

Elena stepped out, meeting Aaron's gaze with an affectionate smile. She appreciated his effort to maintain the illusion, even in front of his cousin. Elena smoothed down her dress and adjusted her necklace, gathering her confidence for what awaited them.

Aaron closed the door and slipped his arm around her waist, pulling her close as they waited for Max's arrival.

Whispering into Elena's ear, Aaron reassured her, "Relax, Elena. We've got this."

She turned to him, offering a smile and nodding in agreement.

"Cousin!" Max hooted as he reached them.

Aaron and Max exchanged a fist bump, their usual greeting. "Good to see you too," Aaron greeted with a grin.

"I wouldn't miss this for anything in the world," Max said, turning his attention to Elena. "You must be the lucky lady."

Aaron growled playfully, tightening his grip around Elena's waist. "Back off, buddy. She's all mine."

Max laughed, clearly enjoying the teasing banter. "Can't blame me for being excited to meet her."

Aaron smiled and chimed in, "Can't trust a player."

Elena joined in the laughter, feeling at ease with Max's friendly demeanor. She hoped the rest of Aaron's family would be as welcoming.

Glancing at Aaron, she hid a smile, appreciating how well he played the role of the perfect boyfriend. It was now up to her to match his performance.

"It's a pleasure to meet you too, Max," she said, returning his grin.

Max grinned back, gesturing for them to proceed. "Let's go. Your mom is waiting for us."

"Just mom?" Aaron asked, surprised.

Max chuckled. "Were you expecting a full entourage?"

Aaron shook his head, feeling a sense of relief wash over him. The evening suddenly seemed a bit easier. "No, I wasn't."

With Max leading the way, Aaron kept his arm around Elena's waist, refusing to let go. He relished the feeling of her in his embrace as they made their way inside.

It seemed that his worries about a large gathering were unfounded. His mom had certainly kept him on his toes, making him think she had invited the entire community. Her ability to surprise him was both exhilarating and endearing.

Together, they followed Max, ready to face whatever lay ahead. Elena knew that this charade was far from over, but as she walked alongside Aaron, she couldn't help but feel a sense of excitement and anticipation for the unexpected moments yet to come.

Elena smiled warmly as she stepped inside the house, taking in the pleasant warmth and delightful aroma that filled the air. However, what warmed her heart even more was the genuine smile on Aaron's mom's face. It was evident that Clara was thrilled to meet her, and Elena couldn't help but notice the striking resemblance between Aaron and his mother. At 5'4" with a petite frame, elegantly styled silver hair, and warm hazel eyes, Clara was a

77

looker. Elena could see where Aaron got his stunning looks from.

"Oh, Elena," Clara cooed as she approached, arms open for an embrace. "It's so wonderful to finally meet you. I couldn't believe it when that mischievous boy told me he was in a relationship."

Aaron chuckled. "See, Mom? I wasn't lying."

Elena smiled, feeling a sense of comfort as she melted into Clara's warm embrace. "Good evening, Mrs. Montgomery."

Clara gently pulled back, shaking her head with a warm smile. "Oh, please, dear. Call me Clara. We're family now." She waved off Elena's attempt at formality, emphasizing the warmth and familiarity they would share.

"This way, my dear," Clara said, leading them further into the house. Elena followed, feeling a mix of excitement and a hint of guilt. As the night progressed and she found herself enjoying the company of Aaron's family, she couldn't help but wish that she wasn't deceiving them.

Over the course of the evening, Elena played her role as Aaron's girlfriend flawlessly. She engaged in conversations with family members, effortlessly navigating through their inquiries and showing genuine interest in their lives. She was careful to strike a balance between being warm and charming, yet not crossing the line into being overly affectionate with Aaron.

At one point during the evening, Aaron's mother approached Elena, a warm smile on her face. "You know, Elena, Aaron has
79

always been a bit of a troublemaker, but there's something different about him when he's with you. I can see how much he cares for you."

Elena's heart skipped a beat, and she couldn't help but glance at Aaron, who was engaged in a conversation with his cousins. She smiled back at Mrs. Montgomery. "Thank you. Aaron means a lot to me too."

In that moment, surrounded by the warmth of Aaron's family, Elena longed for their acceptance and wished that the relationship she was portraying was real. She allowed herself to envision a future where she would genuinely be Clara's daughter-in-law, creating lasting memories with a loving and accepting family.

As the night came to an end and Elena bid farewell to Aaron's family, she couldn't help but reflect on the whirlwind of emotions and the unexpected turn her life had taken. It was a daunting task, pretending to be in love and navigating through this charade, but there was a part of her that felt alive, excited for the adventure that lay ahead.

CHAPTER FIVE

"Thanks for having me," Elena smiled as she bid her goodbyes to Clara and Max, feeling a tinge of sadness that the evening had come to an end.

"Oh, please," Clara grinned, her eyes twinkling with warmth. "Don't make it seem like a sad farewell."

Elena chuckled, amazed at Clara's perceptiveness. "I had an incredible time tonight. Thank you, Clara."

Clara playfully waved off Elena's gratitude. "And you'll have even more fun on Friday."

"Friday?" both Aaron and Elena exclaimed simultaneously.

Clara looked surprised. "What? It's just two days away. Do you already have plans? We can always reschedule if needed."

Aaron groaned, realizing his slip-up. "You've already met my girlfriend, Mom."

Clara huffed, rolling her eyes at her son's reaction. "And I happen to like her. I would have asked you both to stay the night, but since you have work tomorrow, I thought Friday would be perfect. We can have a delightful weekend, bonding and enjoying each other's company. Is that a problem for you, Aaron, keeping your bored old lady company?"

Elena couldn't help but chuckle, witnessing how Clara effortlessly manipulated her son with her charm.

Aaron grumbled, reluctantly giving in. "Friday is fine." He knew the sooner his mother bonded with Elena and let go of the idea of Samantha, the better it would be for everyone.

Clara turned to Elena, her eyes sparkling. "And what about you, my dear?"

Elena smiled, her heart filled with gratitude. "Friday is perfect for me too. I can't wait to see you again, Clara." The thought of spending the entire weekend with Aaron's family meant a significant boost to her finances, and she felt a wave of appreciation toward Clara. She wanted to embrace her in gratitude.

"That's my girl," Clara grinned, bidding them farewell.

"Good job tonight," Aaron said as they settled in the car.

"You too," Elena replied with a sincere smile.

Aaron's smile widened. "Thanks, Elena. You'll see the payment in your account before you go to bed."

"You don't have to thank me. I was simply doing what you're paying me for," Elena replied modestly.

"But I do," Aaron insisted. "Thank you for being available and doing an amazing job. I've never seen my mom as happy as she was tonight."

"She really wants you to settle down. That means you should find yourself a genuine girlfriend soon if you want to keep her happiness intact," Elena teased, nudging him playfully.

Aaron cleared his throat, starting the car. "Let's get you home," he said, the corners of his lips curling up into a smile.

***

"You can't be serious!" Clara exclaimed, her laughter filling the air during Friday evening dinner at her place.

Elena nodded, her eyes sparkling with fondness. "Yes, he was like, 'Be my girl, Elena.' My heart thumped like crazy in my chest that night, and I couldn't help but sway into his arms. The rest of the party was forgotten in that moment."

Clara dabbed at her eyes, her amusement evident. "I can't believe he is such a charmer. I thought he couldn't ask a girl out since he rarely brings them home." She turned to Aaron. "I shouldn't have doubted you, boy."

Elena chuckled, reminiscing about the time Aaron had charmed her off her feet when they first met. "Yeah, he is a true charmer," she agreed, her voice filled with affection.

Clara chuckled, her eyes glinting with nostalgic memories. "Just like his father. Oh, Baron, my sweet darling."

Elena smiled, taking a bite of the delicious food in front of her. "tell me about him. By the way, this food is amazing."

Clara beamed with pride. "Thank you. I can give you my secret recipe. Remind me on Sunday."

"Really? That would be wonderful. Thanks a lot," Elena replied gratefully.

"We were talking about my sweet darling, weren't we? Your father-in-law," Clara continued, a touch of sadness in her voice. "I know he would have liked you too if he was still alive."

The two ladies giggled and smiled, sharing a warm connection as Clara began to share stories of how she had met Aaron's dad.

Meanwhile, Aaron was keenly aware that his mother had spoken some words when she had turned to him, but he couldn't recall exactly what she had said as he hadn't heard her clearly.

His heart had almost stopped when his mother asked Elena how they had met. They had agreed on a story beforehand since Aaron had already told his mother that they had only recently met, but he couldn't help the fear that surged through his veins. He watched and listened intently as Elena proceeded to tell his mom their fabricated story, captivating both of them.

Part of the story Elena told his mom was his idea, but he was amazed at how she embellished it with unexpected twists and shared it with such genuine enthusiasm. Her eyes sparkled as if it were a cherished memory, and for a moment, Aaron found himself almost convinced that it had truly happened that way, if he didn't know better.

He had to remind himself that it was all an act. He needed to get his head back in the game. Even though Elena was sweeping his mom off her feet with her sweetness, he couldn't afford to lose his own footing.

Clara stretched, a mischievous grin on her face. "I'm afraid it's too late for my old bones to keep up with the night. We'll continue tomorrow, dear," she said, directing her smile at Elena. "After all, we have the whole weekend ahead of us."

As they bid each other goodnight and prepared to leave, Aaron turned to Elena with a grateful smile. "Good job tonight," he said appreciatively.

Elena returned the smile. "You too. It was a wonderful evening."

"Thanks for being available and playing your part so well. I've never seen my mom as happy as she was tonight," Aaron expressed his gratitude.

"You don't have to thank me. I was just doing what you're paying me for," Elena replied modestly.

"No, I mean it. It means a lot to me," he insisted. "I want to make sure you know how much I appreciate it.

"Goodnight, mom."

"Goodnight, my dears," Clara replied, her voice filled with warmth. "I've already tidied Aaron's old room for the two of you, so you can go to bed whenever you're ready." With those words, she walked away, leaving Elena feeling a mix of anticipation and unease.

As soon as Clara was out of sight, alarm bells began to ring in Elena's head. She turned to Aaron, her voice filled with terror as she whispered, "Are we sleeping in one bedroom?"

Aaron chuckled, the realization dawning on him. "Were you expecting my mom to get us separate rooms?" He grinned mischievously at Elena.

"Yes," she hissed, her fear and discomfort palpable.

"You're my girlfriend," Aaron reminded her playfully, as if it were the most obvious thing in the world.

"Well we could be practicing abstinence," Elena hissed back, frustrated by his nonchalant response.

He chuckled. "I don't recall that being part of our deal."

Glaring at him, Elena retorted, "That's because I didn't expect us to share a room."

Aaron stood up, moving closer to her. "So, you're confident that you wouldn't be attracted to me while acting as my girlfriend?"

Swallowing hard, her heart pounding, Elena refused to be intimidated. She raised her head, staring defiantly back at him. "Yes, I am."

He snorted and returned to his seat. "Fine. Do as you wish, but I don't want to start explaining to my mom why my girlfriend is scared to share a room with me. It's not like you think I'm going to molest you in the middle of the night."

Elena took a moment to absorb his words, realizing that he was right. They didn't have to engage in any intimate activities, and searching for another room would only raise suspicions she preferred to avoid.

With a sigh, she reluctantly asked, "Where's your room?" The words felt uncomfortable in her mouth, but she knew it was the best option.

"The second door on your left," Aaron replied, his voice tinged with resignation. He observed the look of apprehension in Elena's eyes, understanding her hesitation all too well. The fact that she didn't want to share a room with him hurt him more than he cared to admit. "If it makes you feel any better, I'll take the couch while you have the bed," he offered, hoping to ease her concerns.

A small smile tugged at Elena's lips. "Thanks," she said appreciatively.

95

Aaron snorted, amused by her response. Did she just thank him for giving up the bed? He sighed, realizing that their arrangement had become even more complicated. He pushed aside his half-eaten food, the taste already forgotten in his mouth, despite his mother's delicious cooking.

As Elena stepped into Aaron's old bedroom, she couldn't deny the whirlwind of thoughts and emotions that had raced through her mind upon learning they would be sharing a room. She placed her hand on her chest, feeling a mix of excitement and trepidation.

Her body flushed with excitement, but quickly a wave of horror washed over Elena as she turned to Aaron, desperate to get another room before she embarrassed herself in front of him. She couldn't deny that she was falling for him. Despite her best efforts to convince herself that it was all a lie, the touches, looks, and smiles were starting to get to her.

Even at the office, Aaron had softened towards her, causing her to melt even more. She looked around the room, hoping to distract herself from the sexual tension building within her. Exploring his room would also give her a glimpse into Aaron's personal life, as she doubted she would have another chance once their arrangement came to an end.

Her eyes landed on a stack of papers, and upon closer inspection, she realized they were letters. Curiosity consumed her, and against her better judgment, she opened one. As she read through the letters, her heart sank, and she felt sick to her stomach. They were love letters exchanged between

97

Aaron and another woman. She couldn't bring herself to read any further, and the tears welled up in her eyes.

Regret washed over her, knowing that curiosity had gotten the better of her. If she had known the content of the letters, she would have stayed far away from them. Questions bloomed in her mind and she wondered who the mysterious woman was. The letter had only been addressed as M and she wondered if it was a secret relationship or simply a pet name.

From the way things were, she doubted they were together or she wouldn't be here playing fake girlfriend.

Considering the dates on the letters, it was clear that Aaron had dated her after their own relationship had turned sour. Did he still have feelings for "M"? Had he cheated on her as he had on Elena?

Startled, Elena jumped as the door opened, and Aaron walked in. He immediately noticed the wild look in her eyes and the tension in her body, narrowing his gaze at her.

"What are you doing?" he demanded.

"Nothing," she squeaked, quickly moving toward the bed.

His eyes fell on the open letters, and a scowl formed on his face. "Did you read those letters? Weren't you taught that it's rude to snoop around someone's personal belongings?"

She scoffed, her frustration evident. "I thought I was your girlfriend. Aren't we supposed to be open with each other?"

His nostrils flared, and he stared at her with a mix of exasperation and anger. "So now, you want to play the girlfriend card? Fine. Since you've agreed to be my girlfriend, I guess I don't have to sleep on the couch anymore." He moved towards the bed. "It's your loss if you choose not to sleep."

Elena's heart ached, torn between her feelings for Aaron and the hurt caused by the discovery of those letters. She knew she had to confront him about it, but for now, she couldn't deny the pull she felt towards him, even if it meant facing the painful truth.

"Who is M?" Elena couldn't stop herself from asking, her curiosity and unease consuming her.

Aaron stopped in his tracks and turned to face her. "M is a woman I dated and eventually broke up with."

"Why?" Elena raised an eyebrow, her voice tinged with skepticism. "Did you cheat on her, just like you cheated on me?"

He growled, his anger flaring in his eyes. "No, I didn't cheat on her. We ended things because her father arranged a marriage for her, and she didn't have the courage to defy him. Those letters were my attempt to reach out to her when she stopped answering my calls, but as you can see, they were all returned to me." He sighed, questioning why he was sharing these details with her. Even his mother didn't know much about his past relationship with Marianne.

He rolled his eyes, growing weary. "And just so you know, I didn't cheat on you either," he said, making his way towards the bed. He was tired and simply wanted to sleep.

"You didn't?" Elena's voice croaked with disbelief.

He sighed, turning back to face her. "No, Elena, I didn't cheat on you. You didn't give me a chance to explain that night. That's why I was so angry when you became my personal assistant. I would never betray the trust of someone I love, and you know how much I loved you. The fact that you didn't let me explain shows how little you know and trust me, and it infuriates me."

"Infuriates?" she repeated, her voice filled with remorse.

"Yes, Elena. It infuriates me even after all these years that you easily believed I was a cheat."

"What about Marianne?" she asked, her confusion evident.

He raised an eyebrow. "Is she the issue here?"

"I'm sorry," Elena apologized. "Who is Vera?"

"That's what I'm trying to tell you. I don't know who Vera is, nor have I ever been involved with her."

"But..." Elena furrowed her brow. A day before the night she broke up with Aaron years ago, she had heard someone mention her boyfriend's name as Aaron to her friends, and they had referred to her as Vera. She realized she had overreacted upon seeing that text because of what she had already heard.

Could she have been manipulated? Had someone intentionally orchestrated her breakup with Aaron? She could see the sincerity in his eyes, and she wanted to believe him. Reflecting on the past, she realized how convenient it was for her to hear about Aaron having another girlfriend one day and receiving a text from the same person the next. It seemed unlikely for things to unfold so quickly unless they were planned.

"Is that all?" Aaron sneered at her before retreating to bed.

As Elena watched him drift off to sleep, a heavy sigh escaped her lips. She couldn't help but wonder if she had fallen for a lie and lost out on Aaron because she had been

too impatient to hear him out and trust
him.

CHAPTER SIX

Elena entered the company with confidence, her stride filled with a sense of contentment and a smile gracing her face. She had experienced an incredible weekend, and although things had briefly become awkward when she confronted Aaron about their past, they had swiftly moved past it.

Both of them understood the importance of maintaining their roles for Aaron's mother, so they had apologized to each other and decided not to let the past interfere with the present they had built together. Clara had been a joy to be around, and Elena felt a pang of sadness knowing she wouldn't be seeing her anytime soon. However, with the matchmaking scheme canceled and her acceptance as Aaron's girlfriend, Elena no longer needed to fulfill that role.

But Elena wasn't overly concerned about Clara's absence. After all, she had gained substantial financial benefits from the arrangement, quadrupling her wealth in just a month. Additionally, Aaron had eased up on his tyrannical behavior towards her in the workplace.

"Hi," Ian greeted her with a smile, approaching alongside the rest of their group. "You seem happy."

Damien chuckled. "Someone must have had an amazing weekend."

Elena nodded. "I definitely did."

Allyssa beamed. "It's evident."

Shelly interjected, "Regarding the other day, I hope you and Aaron have resolved everything?"

Elena tensed. She had been avoiding her colleagues for a while after the incident to avoid such questions. Couldn't people just let bygones be bygones? She sighed and shook her head. "There's nothing to resolve. Aaron and I are on good terms."

She noticed their gasps and wide-eyed stares, puzzled as to what she might have said wrong.

"What?" she asked, her confusion evident.

"You called him Aaron," Shelly pointed out.

"Yes, don't we all operate on a first-name basis here?" Elena replied, turning to Allyssa for confirmation.

Allyssa nodded, still looking at her with a mixture of shock and disbelief. "Yes, but you've always referred to him as Mr. Montgomery."

Elena winced as she realized her mistake. Over the past week, she had slipped back into the habit of calling him Aaron, as they had done when they were dating. Moreover, she wasn't as accustomed to using his last name as she was to using his first name.

She let out a nervous chuckle. "Well, as I mentioned, we're on good terms." With that, she hurriedly walked away from their group, hoping to avoid any further slip-ups that might make her feel uncomfortable.

Ian, Damien, Shelly, and Allyssa huddled together, their heads close as they whispered among themselves.

"I knew there was something going on between them," Shelly grinned, thrilled to have found an office gossip topic and to be proven right.

Damien whistled low. "How did you know?"

Shelly beamed, a glow sparkling in her eyes as she launched into telling her colleagues what she believed they could have figured out on their own. It felt good to be smart and observant. She couldn't help but praise herself.

"It was weird that Aaron just hated her when they first met, and Allyssa said that she almost fainted on her first day of work when she heard that her boss's last name is Montgomery. I knew from there that something had happened between them."

Ian grinned, eagerly latching onto the story. "They were probably lovers in the past, but things ended badly between them. That's why they didn't want to work with each other."

"Wow, she should have resigned," Ian chimed in.

Allyssa snorted in amusement. "Do you really think she wouldn't have thought of that? The company pays more than others."

Shelly couldn't contain her excitement and blurted out another piece of news. "I think they're back together."

"What?" Damien asked, his eyes widening with shock. "An office romance between a boss and his assistant? That sounds interesting."

Shelly nodded confidently. "How else do you want to explain the sudden change in their behavior?"

Ian nodded in agreement. "Yeah, she comes out for lunch now with him 21and smiles on her way to work every morning."

"And she used to come to work like she'd rather be somewhere else, but it's different now," added Allyssa.

"Let's see where this goes," Allyssa sighed. She couldn't help but feel relieved that Elena didn't have to dread coming to work anymore, although she was curious to see how the dynamics between Aaron and Elena would evolve.

Elena sighed as she walked into her office, dumped her bag on the desk, and slumped into her chair. She had almost given herself away earlier.

On second thought, she didn't believe she had done anything wrong by showing everyone that Aaron wasn't the bully he had made himself out to be during the incident in the cafeteria. However, she didn't want people speculating about a nonexistent romance between them.

She firmly believed that Aaron shouldn't have let their personal drama spill into the office. They should have kept their disagreements private. He should never have allowed it to become public knowledge.

Glancing at her desk, she noticed that Aaron had already left tasks for her, and a smile formed on her face. That was his way of signaling that he didn't need to come into her office unless it was truly important.

So, this was how they were going to play it. Fine. She must have hurt him with their confrontation during the weekend, and since his mother wasn't around, he didn't want to pretend to get along with her when he didn't feel like it.

Elena was determined to focus on her work and maintain a professional relationship with Aaron. They had a job to do, and she wasn't going to let their personal history distract her.

Elena sighed. Yeah, she deserved that. She had claimed the past was the past, but she had been the first one to throw it in Aaron's face when she had the chance.

Moreover, he had confessed to her that night that she had reopened a wound in his heart - a wound that had never fully healed - with her accusations. She didn't know what to make of his confession that he had never gotten over her, but she pushed her worries aside and focused on her work.

An hour later, the main door to her office opened, and she raised her head, wondering who it could be. It wasn't lunch break yet, and Aaron didn't appreciate employees loitering around during work hours.

Her breath caught in her throat as she stared at him, fear creeping up her spine and goosebumps covering her skin. "What are you doing here Cole?" she wanted to hiss at him, but her voice only came out as a terrified squeak.

He smiled, pleased that he still had an effect on her. "To win you back, baby, and it looks like you still want me."

She hissed, her eyes flashing with anger. "You must be sick, Cole."

"Don't call me sick, baby," he sighed, moving closer to her.

She squeaked, scrambling up from her seat and moving backward. "Baby," Cole moaned, stretching his hand out toward her.

"Don't come closer. Stay away from me," she yelled, her heart pounding and drenched in sweat. She narrowed her eyes at him, contemplating how she could maneuver around him and make a run for it.

But before she could make a move, Aaron's voice cut through the air. "What's going on here?" he growled as he burst out of his office.

His gaze landed on Elena in the stranger's arms, and his anger boiled within him. She looked like a frightened mess, and he couldn't believe that he still felt protective over her.

"Let her go," Aaron gritted through his teeth. "Now."

"And who are you?" Cole raised an eyebrow.

Aaron sneered. "Can't you read the handwriting on the wall, dude? I'm her boss. Let her go and leave."

"Oh, I don't want my girl fired because of me," Cole grinned and released Elena.

She stumbled, and Aaron caught her, shielding her behind him. He despised how broken she seemed and couldn't bear to imagine what she had endured at Cole's hands for her to become so fragile.

He suddenly loathed himself and regretted his prank with his name.

Cole scoffed at Elena. "You know I'll get you back, Elena," he said before walking out of the office.

Elena struggled on her trembling legs, nearly collapsing, but Aaron caught her and guided her back to her chair.

"Thank you," Elena said, smiling gratefully at him.

Aaron frowned, staring at her as she shuddered and fought to regain control. He shook his head, his lips pressed into a thin

119

line, wishing he could have at least thrown a punch at the bastard who had caused such havoc in Elena's life.

"This won't do. Let's get you home," he said. "Let me grab my phone and car keys. Clear out your desk before I return."

Elena nodded, grateful for his support. "Thank you," she whispered as he stepped outside.

"Let's go," he said, leading her out of the office, supporting her with his arms.

Ian and Shelly gasped as they witnessed Aaron and Elena walking out of the company, hand in hand.

Shelly grinned at Ian, feeling a sense of satisfaction. "I told you so."

Ian chuckled, shaking his head. "What a surprise."

***

As Elena sat huddled on the couch, Aaron approached her with a comforting cup of hot tea in his hands. His presence brought a sense of solace, and she couldn't help but appreciate his gesture.

With a grateful smile, Elena accepted the tea from Aaron. "You really didn't have to do this, but I truly appreciate it."

Aaron shrugged, taking a seat beside her. "I couldn't just ignore what happened right outside my office. I couldn't stand by while you were terrified."

Elena's smile widened, touched by his concern. "Thank you. I don't think Cole will come back anytime soon."

"Cole? An ex-boyfriend?" Aaron asked, his curiosity piqued.

Elena nodded, deciding to be honest with him. "Yes, but he was more than just an ex. He was toxic, and that's why I had to move here. I just wish he would let go and move on."

Aaron's gaze softened, understanding the pain in her voice. He reached out and gently wiped away a tear that escaped down her cheek. "I'm sorry you had to go through that. You deserve better."

She gasped as his finger touched her face, sending warm jitters cascading through her belly.

He stared at her, and she held her breath, staring at him as well as she wondered what he wanted to do.

Aaron groaned, feeling his attraction to her rouse to life. He was suddenly overcome with the need to kiss her. It was a burning desire, fueling his arousal till he groaned out loud.

Fires of passion crackled in the air between them, and he couldn't deny that she could feel it as well. He leaned over and placed his lips gently on hers, praying that she wouldn't push him away.

She didn't and he felt joy sing in his veins. He bit down gently on her lower lip, and she moaned, moving closer to him.

He gasped as he realized what he was doing. She had just gone through an emotional moment and might be letting him kiss her to forget about it. She didn't want him and might not even be in her right mind.

He frowned and leaned back. He wanted her and wanted her to feel the same for him and not use him to erase the memory of another man.

"I'm sorry." He apologized and stood up. "I should go."

"Why?" She croaked, staring at him with lust-filled eyes.

He groaned as he glanced at her and felt his arousal getting fuller. He looked away with a sigh. He just couldn't do this.

"Why are you leaving, Aaron?"

"It's just not right that I take advantage of you. I don't want you to add another item to your list of regrets." It would kill him if she regretted making love with him.

She snorted. "who told you that you are taking advantage of me? I wouldn't have kissed you back if I didn't want to."

He turned back to her, allowing hope to fill his heart. "You mean that?"

She grinned. "How about I show you instead?" She stood up and wrapped her hands around his neck, leaning over to kiss him.

He was lost the moment her lips touched his, drowning in the pit of desire as sparks flew between them. He groaned as they grinded against each other, their tongues battling in each other's mouth as they clung to each other.

She trailed her fingers through his scalp, ruffling his hair and he let out a husky groan.

"Elena," he breathed. He had missed this. He had missed her.

"Take me, Aaron." She breathed back. "Love me."

He grinned. "Gladly, my dear." He said and scooped her up, using his instinct to find out where her bedroom was.

He walked into her room, dropped her on the bed and hastily got out of his clothes, watching as she did the same to herself.

There was no pretense or holding back. It was a heated passion burning in them and the only thought was to relieve it.

He kicked his clothes off, hungry for her. This was no slow lovemaking but a fast paced and wild sex between two souls desperate for each other.

They both reached out for each other the same time, sighing with abandon as they fell into each other's arms.

Yes. This was it. Aaron groaned. She felt so right in his arms it was as if she never left.

He sniffed the air, getting harder at the scent of her arousal. She reached over and touched his erection, her finger slightly tracing the tip and he lost it, coating her finger with a slight amount of cum.

"Hmmm," she moaned, raising her finger to her lips and sucked on it.

His eyes went dark and he kissed her, pushing in a finger into her core at the same time.

"Oh!" She gasped, arching her back as a wave of lust swept through her.

This was good. He felt so good that he brought tears of relief to her. She couldn't remember enjoying sex with Cole, she was always so scared she started to avoid him.

It was Aaron who had always brought out the sexy temptress out in her and she was back with him. He felt so good her body took the lead and began to move on its own, leaving her awash and wanton with desire.

He continued to push his fingers into her, playing with and stroking her clit, and stretching her. "You are so freaking tight, baby but already wet for me."

"Still think I don't want you?" She smiled at him. She had been wet for him for days and her body was already singing with anticipation of the release it would be getting.

He chuckled. "I am no longer left with any doubt, baby." He said and guided his erection to her wet entrance, pushing into her.

"Aaron!" She gasped, biting down on her lips as she held on to his back with her fingers.

He waited for her to fully stretch and accommodate him before he began to move.

"Oh!" She moaned as he began to move, his thrusts sending powerful vibrations ricocheting through her.

He thrust, pulling her hips up as he pressed down on her ass, uncaring that she had almost peeled off his back with her nails in her throes of passion.

That was his badge, and he would gladly wear it. He pushed down, his thrusts getting faster as his desire consumed him, loving how she pushed against him as well, meeting him thrust for thrust and heat for heat.

"Elena," he stared at her, etching the moment into his brain and pushed a final time into her.

She melted in his arms, the look he had given her unlocking her orgasm and they were both screaming out their passion at the same time.

CHAPTER SEVEN

Elena looked up as the door to her office opened and a lady entered the room. A radiant Caucasian woman stepped in, her porcelain skin glowing with a flawless complexion.

Her lustrous, flowing golden locks cascaded down her shoulders, framing her striking features with a touch of elegance. With piercing blue eyes that sparkled like sapphires, she exuded an aura of confidence and grace. Her slender figure was draped in a chic and tailored white dress, accentuating her graceful curves as she made her way in, walking confidently as though she had a claim to where she was.

Elena frowned as she gazed at the woman standing before her, her mind racing to figure out who she could be. It was a surprise to see someone unexpected, as she was not aware of any scheduled appointments with Aaron at that particular time. The departure of the last secretary who had briefed her on Aaron's calendar had left Elena solely responsible for managing his appointments.

"Good morning," the woman greeted, her voice a sultry purr that sent a shiver down Elena's spine. The seductive tone made Elena feel uneasy about allowing her access to Aaron. Her mind briefly wandered to the notion of women who used their charms to entice business executives under the guise of having a meeting. However, upon closer observation, the woman did not seem to fit that profile. While she exuded an

undeniable allure and possessed an
intimidating beauty, there was an air of
sophistication and substance about her that
went beyond mere seduction.

Elena considered the possibility that she
might be one of Aaron's business partners,
which would explain her confident
entrance. It was unfair to judge solely based
on appearances, especially as Elena found
herself developing feelings for her boss. She
silently scolded herself for entertaining
such thoughts, reminding herself to
maintain professionalism.

"Excuse me, is Aaron inside?" the woman
inquired, her eyes locked onto Elena's.

Aaron? Elena couldn't help but wonder
how close they were to be on a first-name
basis. She quickly chastised herself,

realizing she was overthinking the situation.

Elena offered a polite smile to the visitor. "Yes, he's inside. Let me inform him of your presence."

The woman waved off Elena's offer, flashing her perfectly manicured red nails in a dismissive gesture. "Never mind. He wouldn't mind," she stated, striding confidently towards Aaron's office without waiting for a response.

Coincidentally, Aaron emerged from his office at that very moment, holding a stack of files. "Elena, could you..." he began, only to be interrupted by a familiar voice calling his name.

"Aaron," the woman said, and his face lit up with delight. "Marianne."

Alarm bells rang loudly in Elena's mind. Marianne? Could this be the same Marianne he had loved and pined for after their breakup? The woman to whom he had poured out his heart in letters that had filled Elena with a mixture of jealousy and longing.

Elena's eyes narrowed as she watched the two of them embrace, her heart filled with a surge of jealousy. She fixated on their joined hands, feeling a searing heat building within her. She scolded herself for succumbing to possessiveness over Aaron, reminding herself that their connection had been purely physical. It was just that, nothing more, and she had willingly entered that arrangement without expecting any emotional attachment.

The intensity of her emotions caught her off guard, leaving her grappling with the

137

realization that her feelings for Aaron ran deeper than she had initially acknowledged.

Yes, they had had sex together but that didn't mean that she could lay a claim to him.

It had been sex, just that and she knew what she had been going into before she had jumped into bed with him or rather, before she had pulled him into bed with her.

They had spent the whole day fucking each other's brains out but that had just been it. Satisfying some primal urge for their bodies to connect and that had ended the moment he had walked out of her apartment.

He hadn't promised her forever and exclusivity, and she wondered why she was getting worked up. Both of them hadn't even discussed about their moment in bed afterwards, they had only lapsed into their normal boss and assistant routine the next day, their moments a secret memory cherished by each of them at their own leisure.

She sighed, taking her eyes away from the duo and turned to her computer.

The annoying thing was that she could hear them and despite herself, she still glanced at them from the periphery of her eyes, even as she typed furiously on the keypads of her computer just to remind them of her presence.

"I missed you, Aaron." She sighed.

Elena rolled her eyes and hit her snort to herself to avoid asking herself why her heart lurched with pain at her words.

Her brows furrowed as she discreetly glanced at the woman before her. She couldn't help but question the situation. Hadn't Aaron mentioned that Marianne was married? What was a married woman doing embracing another man in such intimate manner? Conflicting emotions stirred within Elena as jealousy and confusion waged war in her mind.

She scoffed inwardly at her own thoughts. Aaron wasn't hers to claim, and entertaining such possessiveness would only lead to heartache. But as she observed the intimate moment between Aaron and Marianne, a startling realization dawned on Elena. She was undeniably in love with Aaron.

During their time together over the past week, Elena had found herself drawn to Aaron's genuine kindness and the flickers

140

of the man she had once loved. The connection they had formed went beyond mere physical attraction. She had slept with him not just to satisfy their undeniable chemistry, but because she had fallen for him all over again.

"Darn it," Elena muttered under her breath, chastising herself for falling into this emotional abyss. She had unwittingly walked right into the trap she had been so desperate to avoid – falling in love with Aaron once more.

Aaron's voice interrupted her thoughts, pulling her attention away from their embrace. "Let's go inside," he suggested, disentangling himself from Marianne's hold.

Elena took a deep breath, relieved that their public display had moved out of her sight.

141

However, curiosity lingered in her mind, wondering what would transpire behind closed doors. She feigned indifference, deliberately averted her gaze, and focused on anything but the sight of Aaron and Marianne entering his office.

Hours passed, and frustration etched itself onto Elena's face. Marianne had yet to emerge. Perhaps Aaron had noticed Elena's discomfort, which explained his neglect to request refreshments. She chuckled wryly at her own assumptions, realizing that Aaron was simply avoiding an uncomfortable situation. She needed to stop overthinking things.

Glancing at the clock, Elena's lips pursed in annoyance. Why were they taking so long? Would she spend the entire day with Aaron? Didn't she have work to attend to?

She was unintentionally disrupting Aaron's productivity.

As the door to his office finally opened, Elena's attention snapped back to the pair. Her heart sank when she heard her name being mentioned.

"I'm going home already, Elena. You are free to clear out my schedule and go home as well if you are done."

What? He was going home? With Marianne? She swallowed and nodded, unable to form words past the lump in her throat. Aaron was leaving, and she was free to wrap up his tasks and go home if she wished.

Marianne stared at her and walked off with Aaron, moving closer to him, too close to him.

Elena's throat tightened, making it impossible to respond. Aaron was going home, and Marianne was accompanying him. The proximity between them as they walked together fueled Elena's despair, intensifying her love for Aaron as she struggled to witness him grow intimate with another woman.

Elena sighed heavily, shaking her head in resignation. She contemplated resigning from her position, unable to bear the torment of seeing the man she loved entangled with someone else. Her initial hopes of reigniting their relationship now seemed like an impossible dream. She sighed once more, acknowledging the futility of her endeavors.

Her thoughts were interrupted by the shrill ring of her phone, causing her to jump in surprise. The caller ID displayed an unknown contact, and she furrowed her brow, wondering who it could be. Despite her curiosity, she decided to answer the call.

"Hello?" she spoke cautiously into the phone, her voice tinged with skepticism.

"Elena," the voice on the other end of the line said, and she immediately recognized it as Cole's. A reflexive hiss escaped her lips, unable to contain her annoyance.

"Don't hang up, baby," Cole pleaded, his tone filled with desperation.

"What do you want, Cole?" she sighed, a mix of exasperation and weariness in her voice.

He let out a heavy sigh. "Please, Elena, come back to me. I've changed. I have a new job now, and I won't be traveling as much."

She couldn't help but scoff at his words. As if a change of job would erase the pain and scars he had inflicted upon her. If only he knew that his absence was the only reason she had tolerated their abusive relationship.

He continued pleading, desperation lacing his voice. "I know I hurt you deeply, but I swear I've changed. I mean every word I say, Elena."

She snorted derisively, finding it hard to believe that a leopard could truly change its spots.

"I understand if you don't believe me," he said, his voice tinged with resignation. "But

I won't give up until you see for yourself that I'm sincere. I just want a second chance, Elena." With that, he concluded his plea and ended the call.

Elena let out a heavy sigh as she placed the phone back on the table, her mind swirling with conflicting thoughts. She loved Aaron, but circumstances kept them apart. On the other hand, she wasn't in love with Cole, but rekindling their relationship could provide her with a respite from her longing for Aaron.

She pondered whether Cole's claim of change was genuine or just empty words. Perhaps she could seek Sabrina's opinion and ask her to find out the truth. However, she already knew what her friend's response would be. Sabrina would likely call her foolish for even considering the idea of getting back together with Cole. And truth be told, Elena couldn't help but agree with her friend's sentiment. It would be foolish to use Cole as a distraction to numb her heartache for Aaron.

In the end, she took Aaron's advice and decided to call it a day. A relaxing soak in the bathtub and a nourishing meal seemed like the perfect remedy for her weary mind. Perhaps with some time and self-reflection, she would find the clarity she sought.

CHAPTER EIGHT

Aaron entered the office with a stern expression, his gaze fixed on Elena's desk. He was determined to address her recent change in attitude head-on.

"Good morning, sir," Elena greeted, her fingers swiftly typing on the keyboard.

He scoffed and approached her desk, taking a seat and tapping on it until she paused her typing and looked up at him.

"Is something wrong, sir?" she inquired, her voice laced with curiosity.

He nodded. "Yes, you. What's been going on with you lately?"

She shrugged nonchalantly. "I have no idea what you're talking about."

"Fine. Why do you keep calling me 'sir'?"

She chuckled and raised an eyebrow. "Because you are my boss?"

"Not in that tone, Elena," he winced. "Come on, Elena. What happened between us?"

"Nothing. We just don't have to pretend anymore," she replied, a hint of defensiveness in her voice.

"Pretend? Was the sex pretend too? Were those moans fake? The way you clung to me with your nails? Did you fake your orgasms? Did you pretend when you bent over me and sucked me till I reached climax?" he bluntly asked, his words causing her to flinch.

She winced, feeling exposed and vulnerable. This wasn't how she had envisioned their conversation about their intimate encounter. She didn't want their cherished memories thrown back at her face for the sake of confrontation.

"Aaron, please, let's not go there," she pleaded, her voice filled with a mix of desperation and sadness.

"Then tell me what's going on," he implored. "You've become distant all of a sudden."

"Nothing is wrong, Aaron. Let's not make this more awkward than it already is. We were playing a role, and we played it well. It's time to move on," she explained, attempting to keep her emotions in check.

He scoffed disbelievingly. "A role? Well, get ready to play that role one more time. My mother is hosting a gathering tonight, and she wants to show off her son's girlfriend."

"What?" Elena groaned, her heart sinking. She had hoped they were done with the charade of being a couple. The thought of pretending to be in love with Aaron, while her own heart yearned for him, was becoming increasingly painful.

He sneered. "I'll pick you up at eight."

"Why?" she couldn't help but ask, her voice filled with genuine curiosity.

"Already tired of it? I thought you liked the extra money," he taunted, a hint of bitterness in his tone.

"Aaron," she sighed, her voice tinged with frustration.

"Apparently, one of my mother's friends assumed I was gay because I wasn't seen with a lady or known to be in a relationship. So, my mother, in her pride, boasted about her son having a girlfriend. Now they're all eager to meet her," he explained, his words dripping with sarcasm.

"Oh!" Elena groaned, feeling a mix of resignation and frustration. She exhaled deeply and shrugged her shoulders. "Alright then, a deal is a deal."

Ignoring Elena's response, Aaron made his way to his office. "A deal is a deal?" he thought to himself, feeling a twinge of disappointment. He had hoped for more enthusiasm from her, especially considering how much he had been troubled by her sudden distance. Thoughts of her occupied his mind when he woke up in the morning

153

and worried him before he went to bed at night.

He pondered over what was wrong with him, unable to pinpoint the exact issue. All he knew was that he didn't want Elena to keep giving him the cold shoulder. The connection between them had felt real, at least to him, and he couldn't shake off the feeling that there was something more than just a charade between them.

As he settled into his office chair, he couldn't focus on his work. His mind kept drifting back to Elena and their complicated dynamic. He wondered if she felt the same deep down, if there was a reason behind her sudden detachment.

***

Marianne sat at the dinner table with Clara, graciously welcoming the arriving guests. She had always enjoyed hosting dinners, a trait she had developed during her father's business ventures with Aaron. It was through those meetings that she had met Aaron and felt an immediate attraction towards him. They had shared a secret, fleeting relationship, which had come to an end when she made the unfortunate decision to marry Oscar, driven by her father's wishes. Only later did she realize the extent of Oscar's infidelity and call off the marriage.

Months later, after her failed marriage, Marianne found herself thinking of Aaron and decided to seek him out. She had heard he was still single, unaware of any newfound connection he had formed.

155

Meanwhile, Clara, Aaron's mother, knew Marianne as the daughter of a business associate and had always shown warmth and hospitality towards her, extending an open invitation for dinner whenever she was in town.

Curiosity got the better of Marianne as she inquired about Aaron's whereabouts.

"When is Aaron coming?" she asked Clara, casting a glance towards the door.

Clara chuckled knowingly. "I believe he'll be running a bit late."

Marianne frowned, confused by the delay. "Why?"

"He's picking up his girlfriend," Clara explained.

Marianne's eyes widened in shock, her throat tightening. She had been informed that Aaron was still single. "His girlfriend?" she stammered, struggling to hide her surprise.

"Yes, a sweet and loving girl," Clara replied with affection in her voice.

Anger surged through Marianne, but she maintained a composed facade. She resented the idea of Clara favoring another woman over her. Her plans to rekindle the flame with Aaron and win over Clara's affection were quickly disintegrating.

"Well, well," Marianne managed to say, feigning enthusiasm.

"You'll meet her when she arrives," Clara remarked. "You'll see how adorable she is. I nearly matched him with my friend's daughter until he mentioned having a girlfriend." Clara chuckled. "What a sly and secretive boy I have as a son."

Marianne concealed her snort, doubting she would find any woman by Aaron's side, other than herself, adorable.

A few minutes later, Clara's smile broadened as she spotted Aaron and Elena entering the room hand in hand. Elena clung to Aaron's arm, clearly surprised to see Marianne. She hissed into Aaron's ear, "You didn't tell me Marianne would be here."

"Don't worry about her," Aaron reassured her. "She's a family friend, and that's probably why Mom invited her."

Elena rolled her eyes internally. A family friend who had once been Aaron's love interest. She was told not to worry about Marianne, but how could she not feel uneasy and insecure in her presence? The thought crossed her mind that perhaps she should bring Cole to the party and let Aaron experience a taste of the same discomfort. However, deep down, she knew that Cole wouldn't feel the same level of concern, as it was she who was in love with him, not the other way around.

Aaron, unaware of Elena's true feelings, asked, "Does she bother you?"

Elena lied, her voice strained. "No." She couldn't admit that Aaron's ex made her uncomfortable and insecure. It wasn't as if he would ask Marianne to leave the party, so she had to navigate the evening with a brave face.

Marianne almost burst out laughing as she observed Aaron and Elena, secretly relishing in the knowledge that Clara had been deceived by her son's actions.

She had her doubts about Elena being Aaron's real girlfriend. The way Elena had been ignored at the office, the way Aaron had dismissed her, and the way he had instructed her to clear his schedule and go home didn't align with the behavior of a genuine couple. It seemed more likely that Elena was merely his secretary, paid to pretend to be his girlfriend to avoid unwanted matchmaking attempts.

The realization brought a smile to Marianne's face, lifting her mood from the disappointment she had initially felt upon hearing about Aaron's supposed girlfriend. If Elena was just a pretense, Marianne

believed she still had a chance to seduce
Aaron and make him hers.

As Aaron walked into the room, Marianne
couldn't help but coo and approach him
with open arms. "Oh, Aaron," she
exclaimed, wrapping him in an embrace.
"It's always a delight to see you."

Turning her attention to Elena, Marianne
flashed a smile. "I didn't realize you were
his girlfriend. I would have treated you
better."

Elena returned the smile, but her silence
betrayed her curiosity and wariness. She
wondered what Marianne was up to,
sensing that there was something beneath
the surface.

"Come on in, everyone," Clara, Aaron's
mother, invited.

Aaron placed his hand on Elena's waist, guiding her into the room. He pulled out a chair for her and sat beside her, their connection evident in their smiles, gentle touches, and loving glances exchanged between them.

Clara's friends couldn't help but comment on Elena's beauty. "She is stunning," they remarked.

"I told you so," Clara beamed with pride.

Marianne watched with annoyance as Aaron and Elena shared their affection openly, fondling each other's fingers and exchanging loving looks. Disgust and rage swirled within her. But she knew she had to be patient. She hoped to tell Elena to enjoy the charade while it lasted and savor the fleeting moments because soon enough, Marianne would reclaim her man.

She refused to sit idly by and watch another woman steal Aaron from right under her nose.

CHAPTER NINE

Elena stared at Aaron, her eyes wide with surprise and disbelief. Had she heard him correctly? He wanted to take her out on a date? She couldn't help but feel a flutter of excitement mixed with uncertainty. This was uncharted territory for their supposed fake relationship.

"Are you serious?" she asked, her voice tinged with anticipation.

Aaron nodded, a genuine smile gracing his lips. "Absolutely. I want to take you out and celebrate. You've been amazing these past few weeks, and I want to spend time with the real you, not just the persona we created."

A warmth spread through Elena's chest, and a genuine smile formed on her face. "I'd love to," she replied, her voice filled with genuine enthusiasm.

He took her hand in his and gently pulled her towards the exit. She couldn't deny the thrill of his touch, even if it was part of the act they had been playing. It felt different now, charged with a new energy.

Elena couldn't help but voice her concern. "But Aaron, it's still office hours. What about work and what others might think?"

Aaron chuckled, his eyes twinkling with mischief. "Don't worry about that. The office rumor mill is already buzzing with stories about us. Going out for lunch won't cause any more damage than has already been done."

She arched an eyebrow, surprised that everyone seemed to know about their supposed relationship. "Even the cleaners?"

He nodded, a playful grin on his face. "Even the cleaners. It seems like everyone has their own version of our love story."

Elena shook her head in amusement. "I can't believe this. How did I not know?"

Aaron shrugged. "They probably didn't want you to find out. It's their little secret. But now you know, and it's time to embrace it."

She couldn't help but feel a mix of emotions. On one hand, she enjoyed the attention and affection Aaron showed her. On the other hand, the knowledge that it was all a charade loomed over her.

"But Aaron, what about the fact that our relationship is fake? What if people start believing it's real?" she voiced her concerns.

He looked at her with a reassuring gaze. "Let them think what they want. We know the truth, and that's all that matters. Besides, are you willing to announce to everyone that it's fake?"

Elena shook her head, a smile tugging at her lips. "No, I don't think so."

"Then let's enjoy the perks of this little charade while we can," he said, his voice filled with mischief.

She nodded, feeling a sense of adventure in the air. "Lead the way."

With her hand in his, they walked out of the office together, ready to embark on their pseudo-date. Elena couldn't deny the genuine connection she felt with Aaron, even if the circumstances were unconventional. Perhaps this unexpected turn of events would lead them down a path they never anticipated.

***

Elena watched as Aaron expertly parked the car in a lot in Little Havana. She couldn't help but feel a sense of excitement as they arrived at their destination. Stepping out of the car, she followed Aaron towards the entrance of a café, a smile playing on her lips. They chose a cozy booth and settled in, engaged in conversation while waiting for the waiter to attend to them.

As they perused the menu, Aaron asked with a mischievous grin, "What do you want to eat? Or should we go for their special menu?"

She met his gaze with a playful glint in her eyes. "Let's go for the special menu," she replied.

He chuckled. "You're still as adventurous as ever when it comes to food."

Elena nodded, a hint of nostalgia in her voice. "You know me too well."

Curiosity piqued, Aaron leaned in. "Did you manage to get that recipe from my mom?"

A chuckle escaped her lips. "Oh, so you were listening that night?"

He grinned. "You're not the only one who can read me like an open book."

Their banter was interrupted as the waiter arrived at their table, ready to take their orders. Once the waiter left, Aaron brought up the topic of an upcoming office party.

"Will you be my date to the office party, Elena?" he asked, his tone light.

She teasingly raised an eyebrow. "Would you have gone with someone else? I'm pretty sure my loyal supporters in the office would have revolted."

He chuckled, playing along. "Oh, I wouldn't dare risk the wrath of your fans. I'll tread carefully."

Elena smiled, enjoying their playful exchange. "Don't worry, I'll make sure they go easy on you."

171

Their food arrived, filling the air with delicious aromas. As they began to eat, the atmosphere shifted, and Aaron's demeanor turned more serious. Elena couldn't help but notice the change.

"I don't want you to go with me because it's expected or obligatory," he began, his voice earnest. "I want you to be there with me because you genuinely want to be."

Her heart skipped a beat, and she felt a lump forming in her throat. She sensed that he was trying to convey something important, and she eagerly awaited his next words.

"I want to be with you because I genuinely want to be with you," he continued, his gaze unwavering.

Elena's breath caught in her throat. The words hung in the air, laden with meaning and vulnerability. She wanted to hear more, to know what he truly felt, but she held back her own emotions, refusing to jump to conclusions.

"Yes," she finally replied, her voice filled with a mix of hope and anticipation. "I will be your date."

A smile spread across Aaron's face, and he reached across the table to gently press her hand. "Thank you," he whispered.

In that moment, Elena couldn't help but feel a surge of happiness. The future was uncertain, but they were taking steps forward, exploring the possibilities that lay between them. As they continued their meal, their hands intertwined, Elena couldn't help but wonder what adventures

173

awaited them on this journey they were embarking on.

***

Later in the day, Aaron entered his apartment with a whistle, his heart filled with excitement. The source of his joy was none other than Elena. He found himself eagerly anticipating any opportunity to be in her presence, yearning for moments where he could hold her close and see her radiant smile as if he were the center of her world.

Inviting her to lunch earlier had been a way to rekindle the easy camaraderie they shared, to witness her laughter uninhibited and carefree as it used to be when they spent time with his mother. He longed to break through the professional facade she wore at the office and bask in the warmth of her genuine self. He wanted to be the reason behind her laughter, the one who could make her smile effortlessly.

As he reached up to loosen his tie, a sudden realization hit him like a bolt of lightning. He was undeniably in love with Elena once again. He couldn't pinpoint exactly when or how it had happened, but he knew deep in his heart that his feelings were real this time, surpassing the pretense of their previous relationship.

His thoughts were interrupted by the ringing of his phone, jolting him back to reality. Surprised by the late-night call from Marianne, he fumbled to find his phone, wondering what could be the reason for her reaching out at this hour.

"Hi, Marianne," he greeted, concern lacing his voice. "What's the matter?"

She whined on the other end. "Aaron."

Furrowing his brow, he couldn't help but worry about her, sensing something amiss. "What's wrong?"

She let out a laugh. "I just felt like hearing your voice Aaron."

Relieved, he chuckled. "You had me worried there for a moment. Find something to do to pass the time if you're bored."

Marianne continued to tease. "Why were you so quick to worry? Would you have come running if I were in real trouble?"

He chuckled. "I wouldn't have just run to you like that."

176

"Why?" She sneered. "Because you now have a girlfriend?"

Aaron laughed, puzzled by her comment about having a girlfriend. "I know you can handle yourself. You're strong."

"Sometimes, even strong girls need their men, no matter how capable they seem."

He contemplated her words. "Then ask your man to come running to you."

She snorted. "If I had a man, would I be asking you?"

He sighed, concerned about her well-being. "What happened with your husband?" He had refrained from asking during their previous encounter, not wanting to appear inquisitive.

"He cheated on me," she revealed.

Aaron winced; empathy evident in his voice. "I'm sorry to hear that."

"Thanks."

"Are you sure you're only bored and not feeling a bit down as well?" he inquired, sensing there might be more to her current state.

Marianne chuckled playfully. "Maybe I am, maybe I'm not."

A smile formed on Aaron's face. "I think I have a way to help. There's a party coming up soon at my workplace. You should come. Maybe it will lift your spirits."

Her smile brightened. "I think I will. Thank you, Aaron," she said, ending the call. If only he knew that he had unwittingly played into her plans to separate him from his loving, yet fake,

178

girlfriend. He would never have extended the invitation.

***

Elena entered the hall with Aaron, her smile widening as her colleagues erupted in applause and playful cheers. She blushed at their enthusiastic response, feeling like a spectacle as they acted like giddy schoolgirls witnessing their friend talk to her crush for the first time.

Allyssa chuckled beside her. "Go, Elena."

Shaking her head, Elena glanced towards her colleagues, a mixture of embarrassment and amusement washing over her. She understood that Aaron held a legendary status within the company, and many of the female employees harbored feelings for him. But she didn't want to be treated as if she had achieved something extraordinary by dating him. It was both overwhelming and embarrassing.

Aaron leaned closer and whispered in her ear, his voice warm and affectionate. "You look beautiful tonight, baby. I can't express it enough."

Cameras flashed, capturing the moment, and Elena smiled for the photos, although a pang of uncertainty tugged at her heart. She wondered if Aaron's words held true sentiment or if they were merely part of the charade they were playing.

As she scanned the room, her eyes landed on Clara, who approached them with a smile that exuded genuine affection. Elena hoped that Clara's gaze wouldn't turn icy if she ever learned that Elena and her son had ended their relationship.

"My darlings!" Clara cooed, enveloping both Aaron and Elena in a warm hug.

"Mom," Aaron groaned, playfully struggling to free himself from her tight embrace.

"What?" Clara snapped at him. "Can't a mother hug her son at an office party? I come here every year and embrace you, so I don't understand why you're being fussy."

Elena chuckled, appreciating Clara's maternal affection. "He doesn't want the junior employees to witness his softer side."

Clara snorted, unimpressed by Aaron's resistance, and turned her attention to Elena, cradling her face in her hands. "Oh, you poor thing. How do you put up with him? It's a good thing you met and fell in love with him at that party before working for him, or he would have intimidated you too."

Elena smiled, feeling a sense of warmth and acceptance from Clara. "He doesn't intimidate me at all."

Clara beamed. "That's what a woman who loves and trusts her man would say." She patted Aaron on the shoulder. "Enjoy your evening, my darlings. I'll go mingle with the rest of the party."

Aaron chuckled. "Have fun, Mom."

Clara called out, her voice booming across the room as she walked away. "You bet I will, son!"

Aaron winced, slightly embarrassed by his mother's exuberance, but he couldn't help but chuckle. "Mom..."

Elena interjected, her voice light. "Your mom is fun."

He chuckled. "Just wait until you get to know her better."

Elena gazed at him, a hint of sadness creeping into her eyes. The agreed-upon time to end their fake relationship was drawing near, and there wouldn't be an opportunity to truly get to know Clara on a deeper level. Time was running out, and she couldn't help but wish for more moments like these.

CHAPTER TEN

Aaron's grip tightened around Elena's waist, drawing her closer as Marianne approached them. He couldn't ignore the discomfort Marianne's presence caused Elena any longer. The cold shoulder he had received after their encounter in his office had made it clear that Elena was wary of Marianne's intentions.

"Hi, Aaron," Marianne beamed, her eyes narrowing at the sight of Aaron's hand on Elena's waist. "Thanks for inviting me. I'm really having fun."

Aaron shrugged nonchalantly. "It's just a party. I'm glad you're enjoying yourself."

Marianne turned her attention to Elena. "Oh, Elena."

"Hi," Elena responded, offering a polite smile. Deep down, her instincts warned her not to fully trust Marianne, and she couldn't shake the feeling of discomfort in her presence.

"How's the party going?" Marianne inquired. "Having fun?"

"We just arrived," Elena replied.

Marianne chuckled. "Trust me, you're in for a good time."

Aaron swiftly steered Elena away, excusing themselves from Marianne's company. "I'm afraid we have to end this here, Marianne. I have some people to greet before the party starts."

"Okay. See you soon," Marianne replied with a smile.

"Don't wait for me and just have fun, Marianne," Aaron said, his tone indicating their conversation had reached its end.

Marianne chuckled in response. "Oh, you can count on it, Aaron." With a laugh, she walked away.

Aaron didn't dwell on Marianne's cryptic remark. Instead, he guided Elena towards the company's top investors and clients, focusing on the task at hand.

"Does she still bother you?" Aaron asked, his concern evident in his voice.

She smiled, appreciating his consideration. Had he walked away from Marianne because of her? The thought warmed her heart. "Not really," she replied. However, she couldn't shake off her reservations about attending the meeting with investors and clients as his date.

She turned to him, her eyes filled with uncertainty. "Are you sure it's okay for me to be there when you meet with the investors and clients?"

He smiled reassuringly. "You're also my personal assistant, Elena. I'm sure they wouldn't mind."

While his words were true, Elena couldn't help but worry about the potential complications of being introduced as his girlfriend, given their impending breakup. She wanted to avoid any future complications and awkward encounters.

Aaron paused, contemplating her words. He understood her concerns and didn't want to put her in an awkward position.

"You're right," he said, a hint of regret in his voice. "It might be better if you mingle with the other guests. I'll find you afterwards."

Relief washed over Elena as she nodded in agreement. It was a relief to know he understood and respected her perspective. She smiled and lightly squeezed his hand. "Thank you for understanding."

He leaned in, planting a soft kiss on her cheek. "I'll join you soon, okay? Enjoy yourself." Elena blushed, begging her heart to calm down as she stared at his retreating figure. She suddenly needed a drink to distract herself from the feel of his lips on hers. Her lips tingled from where he had kissed her, and she hoped the feel of the cold glass would wake her up.

Needing a moment to compose herself, Elena took a glass from a passing waiter and retreated to a quiet corner, observing the crowd. She hoped a drink would help calm her racing heart and clear her mind. But her moment of solitude was short-lived as Marianne approached her, emitting a palpable aura of hostility.

"I must say, I admire how you work," Marianne hissed, her words dripping with disdain.

Elena glanced at her from the rim of her glass, her curiosity piqued. "What are you talking about?"

Marianne's eyes flashed with hatred as she continued, her voice laced with venom. "Don't pretend like you don't know what I'm talking about, you bitch. Aren't you satisfied with fooling his mother? Now,

190

you're trying to fool the entire world as his girlfriend?" She snorted with contempt. "You think someone like you could ever be his girlfriend?"

Elena's eyes narrowed, a flicker of anger igniting within her. She glared back at Marianne, refusing to let her words go unanswered. "You don't know the half of what you are talking about," she retorted, her voice firm and resolute.

Marianne scoffed. "Can you ever be his girlfriend?" She moved closer to Elena and glowered. "How much did Aaron pay you to pretend to be his girlfriend so you could fool his mom?"

"What did you just say?" the piercing sound of Clara's voice cut through the air, causing both Elena and Marianne to freeze in their tracks. Elena winced, knowing that Clara had overheard their heated exchange and shrunk when saw the expression on Clara's face. Just what she was trying to avoid.

Elena could feel the weight of Clara's gaze upon her, a mixture of pain and disappointment. She had never intended to hurt Clara and seeing her look so heartbroken only intensified Elena's feelings of guilt.

Marianne had walked away, leaving Elena and Clara alone. Clara's eyes gleamed with a mix of anger and curiosity as she confronted Elena with a barrage of questions.

"Is what she said true?" Clara's voice quivered with emotion. "Did Aaron pay you to deceive me? Have you both been lying to me? Are you really my son's girlfriend?"

Elena let out a heavy sigh, her own eyes welling up with tears. She felt a lump forming in her throat as she tried to compose herself before speaking.

"I'm sorry, Clara," Elena managed to say, her voice filled with remorse. She instinctively grabbed her bag and hurried towards the exit, desperately hoping to escape the pain that threatened to overwhelm her.

As Elena fled, Clara stood there in shock, witnessing the girl she had grown to care for running away, tears streaming down her face. In that moment, Clara realized that Elena's pain mirrored her own. Despite the hurt, Clara could sense Elena's genuine regret, a sign that Elena cared just as deeply.

Determined not to let Aaron's actions go unchecked, Clara's anger surged within

193

her. She marched toward where Aaron stood, her fury burning brighter with each step. It was time to confront her son about the repercussions of his reckless decision.

"Aaron!" Clara hissed, her voice laced with resentment as she reached his side.

Startled, Aaron turned to face his mother, a perplexed expression on his face. He couldn't understand why she seemed so upset. The last time he had seen her, they had been looking forward to a joyful evening. Something had clearly changed, and Aaron wondered what could have gone wrong.

"Mom," Aaron began, his voice trembling with a mix of concern and apprehension.

Clara's piercing glare evoked memories of their past disagreements, causing Aaron to question what he had done to elicit such a reaction. He chuckled nervously, trying to ease the tension and remind himself of his mother's propensity for dramatic displays.

However, Clara's anger burned fiercely. Glaring at Aaron as if she could scorch him with her gaze, she uttered words filled with resentment and disbelief.

"Don't you dare 'mom' me!" Clara hissed, her voice seething with intensity. "Is Elena truly your girlfriend? Did you pay her to act as your girlfriend?"

Aaron's heart skipped a beat, and he froze in place, stunned by Clara's accusations. The shock was evident on his face as he struggled to process what she was saying.

"Where did you hear that?" Aaron asked, his voice barely above a whisper, his mind racing to understand how such rumors could have surfaced.

Clara moved closer, her anger palpable as she narrowed her eyes, staring directly into Aaron's. She couldn't believe that he would stoop so low, betraying both her and the girl who was now in tears.

"I overheard Marianne," Clara replied, her voice filled with righteous anger. "She insinuated that you paid Elena to deceive me, to deceive all of us. Is it true?"

Aaron ran his hand through his hair, frustration evident in his voice as he cursed softly. "Mom, I promise I'll explain everything later, but I truly love Elena. You have to believe me."

Clara gasped, her expression a mix of surprise and concern. "You do? Then why did she run away?"

"Who?"

"Elena. She ran out crying."

"Fuck." Aaron cursed.

"Watch your language, boy." Clara warned him.

Aaron cursed under his breath, realizing the impact of Elena's hasty departure. He needed to find her and make things right.

"I need to find Marianne," Aaron muttered, his frustration boiling over. Determined to uncover the truth, Aaron set off in search of Marianne. He spotted her before his mother could respond, her smug smile infuriating him further. He approached her with a hardened expression, his fists clenched at his sides.

Marianne greeted him with a teasing tone. "Hi there. Knew you'd come looking for me."

"What did you do?" Aaron growled, his anger barely contained. "Was this your plan all along?"

Marianne shrugged, an air of victory in her demeanor. "I simply got rid of the misfit between us. Let's not pretend that you're with her because you can't get over me."

Aaron snorted, a mix of frustration and truth in his voice. "If only you knew that I was with you to try and forget about Elena. I couldn't move on when she broke up with me."

Marianne gasped, her confidence wavering. "You can't be serious, Aaron."

"I'm dead serious, Marianne," Aaron sneered. "You think you know everything, but you know nothing. I knew Elena before you, and I never would've been with you if she hadn't left me."

Watching as Marianne's lips trembled, Aaron felt an odd sense of satisfaction. She had prided herself on knowing the truth, and now she needed to face the full extent of it.

Running a hand over his face in frustration, Aaron sighed heavily. "You've just ruined everything."

"Just as you ruined mine!" Marianne screamed, her voice filled with anger. "I came back here for you."

"Did I ask you to?" Aaron glared at her, his patience wearing thin.

"I won't let her have you," Marianne hissed, her eyes narrowing.

Aaron met her gaze with determination. "Let's see you try."

With that, he stormed out of the hall, racing towards his car. His mind was in turmoil as he sped towards Elena's apartment, desperate to find her.

"Elena!" Aaron called out urgently, frantically ringing the doorbell and knocking on the door simultaneously.

Elena opened the door, startled by his sense of urgency. Before she could react, he rushed past her, refusing to be pushed away. His eyes widened as he took in the sight before him—tissues littered across the room, evidence of her tears.

Turning to face her, he felt a pang of guilt. She looked utterly worn out, her eyes puffy and bloodshot.

"Elena," Aaron whispered, his heart aching for her.

He moved closer to her and pulled her into his arms, attempting to comfort her. "I heard about what happened tonight. I'm so sorry, Elena."

She pulled away from his embrace and shook her head, her expression filled with resignation. "There's nothing to be sorry for. Marianne spoke the truth."

Aaron let out a pained groan, her indifference cutting deeper than Marianne's unwarranted jealousy. "Elena..."

She sighed, her voice tinged with weariness. "It's all right, Aaron. We were going to tell your mom about our breakup eventually. Marianne just expedited the process."

"But I didn't ask her to do that. I should have given her a piece of my mind before coming here. She had no right to hurt you the way she did," Aaron expressed, his frustration evident.

Elena sighed, a sense of finality in her words. "But she did hurt me, and it made me realize something. It's time for us to end this charade of a relationship. I don't want to continue living a lie and deceiving everyone I know."

He stared at her, desperately hoping she was joking. But her serious expression crushed his hopes, and he groaned, feeling the weight of the night pressing upon him far too soon.

"We don't have to end our relationship, Elena. I genuinely like you," Aaron pleaded, baring his feelings for her.

She snorted, dismissing his claim. "You like Marianne, Aaron. Don't lie to make me feel better. I don't feel as bad about what happened as you think. I've cried and moved on," she said, gesturing towards the scattered tissues on the floor.

He scoffed at her assertion, finding it hard to believe she could be so sure of his feelings for Marianne. Was she a mind-reader?

"I do like you, Elena, and I mean it. Let's not break up. Can you give me a second chance? Let me show you how much I truly care about you," Aaron implored, hoping to change her mind.

She yawned, exhaustion weighing heavily upon her, and covered her mouth with her hand, trying to hold back more tears. He shouldn't play with her emotions just to avoid admitting the truth to his mom.

"I'm tired, Aaron. Can we talk about this another time?" Elena requested wearily.

Aaron sighed as he was ushered out of her apartment, realizing that he had ended up back at square one—trying to convince Elena to be with him.

He knew Marianne wouldn't give up easily, but he wouldn't give up on Elena either. Regardless of the obstacles, he was determined not to lose her again and prove his genuine intentions towards her.

He had made his choice, and he would give it his all until Elena chose him too as well.

As Aaron walked away from Elena's apartment, a sense of determination filled his heart. He knew he had to find a way to make things right and win her back. Deep down, he couldn't imagine a life without her.

But little did he know that another unexpected twist awaited him just around the corner. As he turned the corner, his phone buzzed with an incoming call. Curiosity piqued, he answered it, only to be greeted by a voice he never expected to hear.

"Marianne," he whispered, his heart pounding in his chest. The unexpected call sent shivers down his spine, leaving him wondering what game she was playing now.

To be continued...

Made in the USA
Middletown, DE
05 June 2023